Scarlet Toys

Violent Circle: Book One

S.M. Shade

Cover art by Ally Hastings at Starcrossed Covers.
Interior formatting by Angela at That Formatting Lady.

Where to find S.M. Shade:

I have a private book group where no one outside of the group can see what you post or comment on. It's adults only and is a friendly place to discuss your favorite books and authors. Drama free. I also host an occasional giveaway, and group members get an early peek at covers, teasers, and exclusive excerpts.

You can join here:
https://www.facebook.com/groups/694215440670693

You can also follow or friend me on Facebook:
https://www.facebook.com/authorsmshade

Or like my page:
https://www.facebook.com/smshadebooks

Chapter One

Cassidy

Have you ever had a day where it feels like you're holding a stick and everyone around you looks like a piñata? That pretty much describes my attitude today. After two years of working at the Crunchy Time Cookie Factory, I've been let go. Well, the word they used was terminated, but it boils down to the same.

Fired.

Canned.

Tossed out on my narrow ass.

I didn't do anything wrong and it's not just me. They're moving the whole operation out of the country so a good portion of our small, southern Indiana town is now unemployed. Which means finding a new job will be even harder since I'm competing with about four hundred other newly unemployed former coworkers.

Fantastic.

I have a small amount of savings to see me through the next two months at most, but at the moment I'm relieved I was able to save that much.

My car chugs and wheezes into the parking spot in front of my apartment. It takes a few seconds for the engine to stop when

I turn it off, and I shake my head. Yeah, my car runs so well it doesn't want to stop. Unfortunately, it doesn't want to stop at lights or stop signs either, but that's another problem.

Two of my neighbors sit outside in lawn chairs, and they give me a wave as I walk by. "I heard about the factory. They're bastards," Samantha calls.

Samantha has lived beside me since I moved in. She's about ten years older than me and we get along well. She's nice, but she gets a lot of crap from others—mainly women—because she...how can I put this? She has a very popular vagina. Seriously, if penises had wings, her crotch would be an airport. I'm not a fan of slut shaming. If men can sleep around, I don't see why women can't. Besides, it's not anyone's business anyway.

"Thanks. I guess I'll be job hunting on Monday."

"Check out the old dollar store building. They have a now hiring sign up," Neal says.

Neal lives across the street with his ten-year-old daughter. He's the only single father in our shitty little neighborhood and it's hilarious to watch the women go after him. So far, he hasn't shown any interest in anyone.

I pause to ask, "What kind of business is opening up there?"

"No idea. They have the windows blacked out. The sign says open interviews tomorrow, though."

"Thanks, I'll check it out."

"Don't forget about the bonfire tomorrow night!" Samantha calls as I head inside.

"I'll be there."

I've lived here in Orchid Apartments on Violet Circle for a few years. It's far from a typical neighborhood. More like an insane asylum poured out into the street. Someone has written an N on the street sign in between the e and t, so it reads Violent Circle, which isn't altogether false. We have our share of violence, as most poor neighborhoods do, but it's not like drive-by shootings or anything. These are the cheapest apartments in town and are also subsidized by the government, so those who don't have a job or who live on disability stay for next to nothing.

It's not a terrible place to live once you get used to it. The people are eccentric at best and petty criminals at worst, but we're all in the same boat and generally have one another's back. I've heard the talk through town. They call it the slums, but what the hell do well off people know about struggling? I'll take honest flaws over fake smiles any day.

I'm met by a wall of heat when I let myself in my little one bedroom apartment. I've put off turning on the air conditioning to save money and I need to do that now more than ever so I open the windows and crank up the fan instead.

Stripping off my clothes as I make my way to the bathroom, I turn the shower on and step under the cool spray, washing away the sweat of the day. At least I won't be spending the day around ovens anymore or end up covered in sugar. Who knows what I'll be doing next though? There are only two factories in town, a supercenter, a few gas stations, and a few fast food restaurants. Fast food is my last choice—the pimples alone aren't worth it—but it may come to that.

Chances are it's some kind of restaurant opening up in the old dollar store building too. I can't count how many have tried to open little family run ice cream parlors, diners, and bakeries here only to have them close down again after a few months. I need something I can count on. Maybe the new liquor store? Our county only went wet this year so the place is pretty new. They may have an opening.

When I'm clean and cooled off, I hop out, wrap a towel around myself and head to my bedroom. Perk number one about living alone; you can walk around naked any time the mood strikes you. It almost makes the chances of slipping in the tub, cracking your head and being found naked, dead, and alone worth it. I've lived with roommates in the past. I'll take the chance of posthumously mooning a maintenance man.

It's still hot as hell in my place so I throw my hair up in a ponytail, dress in some cotton shorts and a tee, and sit out on my step. The air is beginning to cool down and the delicious smell of meat being grilled makes my mouth water. I should go make something to eat, but I'm exhausted, not just from work, but from the stress of being fired.

A patrol car rolls through like they do every night and the cop waves at me. They pretty much know everyone and are aware of the troublemakers. Unless you're hurting someone or stealing, they don't pay any attention. Which is why I don't hesitate to pull a joint from my pocket and spark up.

I don't smoke weed often; usually once or twice per week at most, but tonight I need something to calm my nerves and distract me. There are some serious potheads living here, people who probably piss green, and the smell of weed will most likely attract them like a line of ants, but I don't mind sharing.

As if they heard my thoughts, the neighbors who live next to Samantha—two doors down from me—pop around the corner. Dennis and his wife, Mallory, approach and Mallory takes a seat beside me on the step. When I talked about bleeding green? Yeah, these two are who I had in mind. I've known some smokers, but these two take the cake—or the brownie.

"I heard about Crunchy Time. Sorry you lost your job," Dennis says.

"Thanks," I reply, taking a puff and passing it to him.

"Any idea what you're going to do?"

"Not really. I've only known for a few hours, though."

"Well, let us know if you need anything," Mallory says.

"Thanks, I appreciate it. Just let me know if you get an opening at Rock Plastics." I know it's useless. It's one of the easiest jobs in town and the turnover is almost zilch.

"Will do," Dennis agrees.

We sit in comfortable silence for a few minutes, finishing off the joint. I watch the smoke swirl up in the evening air, taking some of my stress with it.

"Shit. I'm gonna burn the burgers!" Dennis announces, and Mallory and I burst into giggles at the sight of him trying to run his chubby ass around the corner.

"Would you like to eat with us tonight? We have plenty. It's just hot dogs and hamburgers, but..." She shrugs.

See what I mean? There are people who avoid this place like the plague, but most of us are decent, caring people.

"I'd love to, thanks. Give me just a sec, yeah?"

"Come on over when you're ready." Mallory gets to her feet and disappears around the corner of the building.

I was raised never to go to someone's house for dinner without bringing something. I don't have a lot to choose from, but I grab a couple bags of chips and three cans of Coke. Between that and the weed, I don't feel like a mooch.

We eat at the little plastic table in their backyard while they fill me in on the high jinx I missed in the neighborhood today.

"Mantrum was at it again," Mallory says, and I smile around a bite of hot dog. Grilled hot dogs are absolutely amazing when you're stoned.

"Yeah? Cops get called?" Mantrum is the nickname someone came up with for the man who lives across the street. He's in his thirties, but throws tantrums like a child, stomping around, throwing things, and slamming doors. Man tantrums. I can't count the times the cops have been called, but they never take him, just warn him to get back inside and quit being disruptive.

"Not this time. His girlfriend drug him back inside."

"He's eventually going to get locked up if he isn't careful. Cops will get sick of being called to their address."

"I know. More than one of us has tried to reason with him. No one wants to see him get evicted when they have all those kids."

Yeah, four kids under six years old. Five if you count Mantrum.

"Never a dull moment," I reply, shaking my head. "You coming out for the bonfire tomorrow night?"

"Most likely. I get off work at five." Mallory works at the local nursing home as an aide.

I polish off my hot dog and get to my feet. "I'll see you there then. Thanks for dinner."

"Anytime."

I wouldn't usually go to bed so early on a Friday night, but I'm worn out and I want to be up early to job hunt in the morning. A lot of my former coworkers will probably wait until Monday to start looking, so maybe I can beat them to something. I guess the old dollar store building will be my first stop.

The sounds of the neighborhood filter through my open window as I try to doze off. Mallory and Dennis are discussing something, their voices climbing. It's likely to turn into a full scale argument since they generally have a screaming match once a week or so. Samantha is talking on her cell, her occasional laughter flowing into the night.

At least the neighbor right next to me, the only one I share walls with, isn't home. He likes to sing gospel music late into the night sometimes.

The clang and bang of the nearby train yard continues as usual, along with the occasional dog barking. When I first moved here, the noise drove me crazy, but now it's become normal and just lulls me to sleep.

The last thing I hear before I fall asleep is Mallory shriek, "Like I give a shit, you limp dick motherfucker!"

Ahh. The sounds of home.

The patter of rain against the roof wakes me, and I reach over to close the window before the floor gets soaked. A rumble of thunder tells me it probably isn't going to stop anytime soon so I rush to close the rest of the windows.

A giggle escapes me when I see a pile of clothes in the yard in front of Mallory's. They must've really went at it after I left last night if she tossed Dennis's clothes out again. Sometimes, I'm really glad to be single. All I have to do is look around me and be reminded that relationships suck. I'd much rather watch the drama play out than be a part of it.

The rain lets up a little by the time I leave, but there's a small river of muddy water streaming down the street to the sewer drain. Some of the neighbor kids are splashing in it and I have to slow down to drive around them. Damn, what I'd do to have those carefree days back.

As Dennis said, a sign advertising open interviews hangs on the door of the old dollar store, with directions to come to the back door. It is a little strange to see the front window blacked out, but I don't hesitate to head around back.

The door is open and a small table has been set up with a few chairs, all empty except for one.

My jaw nearly hits the floor at the sight of the man who gets to his feet to greet me. He towers over me, easily six foot five, and his broad shoulders and chest flex beneath his suit, clearly outlining muscles that must take endless work at the gym.

Bright, copper colored eyes meet mine and he smiles, extending his hand. "Good morning. I'm Wyatt Lawson."

I'm frozen in place, taking in the glorious piece of man meat standing in front of me. I guess karma decided to cut me a break. Losing my job at the factory was totally worth being in this man's presence. His lips press together and one of his eyebrows begins to journey up his forehead. "And you are?"

Why is he looking at me like that? Does he think I'm attractive? Is he imagining throwing me down and ripping my clothes off? Because that's all I can picture. Clawing his back while he grabs my ass…

Oh, he asked me a question, didn't he? "Ass!" I blurt, and feel my cheeks fill with fire. "Cass," I correct. "My name is Cassidy West."

Please let a sinkhole open under me, or a tornado show up to suck me out of a window. Anything to get me out of this room right now.

Amusement is stamped on his face, his gorgeous, stubbly face, as he gestures toward the chair across from him. "Nice to meet you, Cassidy. Please, have a seat and tell me about yourself."

Trying to resist the urge to give him the real information I want him to have about me, like how I'm on birth control and can give one hell of a blow job, I take a seat and proceed to stammer like a nervous teenager talking to a crush.

"Okay, um, I'm 21 years old. I have a high school diploma and I've worked the past two years at the Crunchy Time cookie factory. Before that, I was a cashier at the supercenter for almost three years. Um, no criminal record and I'm not crazy or slow, regardless of how I might appear at the moment," I babble.

His smile morphs into a laugh as he sits back in his seat and crosses his legs, resting his ankle on his knee.

"That's good to know."

"Sorry, I guess I'm nervous." Maybe because I didn't expect to be interviewed by a fitness model.

"No need to be nervous. Why did you leave your last job?"

"They laid me off along with about four hundred other people. You're probably going to be drowning in applicants."

Getting to his feet, he grins down at me. "We should move this along then. I'm sure you're curious what position you're interviewing for."

Missionary, doggy, whatever, I'm down.

"Yes, of course."

"Follow me."

He leads me through the stockroom and out onto the sales floor where boxes are scattered from hell to noon. "I'm looking for a full time manager, though I'll also be hiring a few hourly employees as well."

He opens a box, and my mouth falls open when he holds up the contents. A giant purple dildo, packaged in a thick plastic case.

"Um, if that's part of the interview, I might be in the wrong place." The whole thing makes me feel like I'm on one of those stupid hidden camera shows. He's setting up a sex toy store? In this little backward town that couldn't even sell alcohol until recently? No way.

"This is what you'll be selling. Sex toys for men and women, lingerie, party supplies, X-rated DVDs, and so on. It obviously isn't a job for everyone so if you aren't interested, please let me know now."

It may be my imagination, but I sense a flicker of disappointment when I don't answer him straight away. He returns the dildo to the box and eyes me.

"Do you have a moral compunction against these types of goods?"

My fingers creep up to tug on my earlobe, a nervous habit

I've been trying and failing to break since childhood. If he saw the array of do-it-yourself devices in my nightstand drawer, he wouldn't ask that question. Now I'm picturing him in my bedroom. Keep it together, Cass.

"No, it's not that, it's just...I'm not sure how long a business like this will survive in Morganville."

A smile brightens his face, showing a mouth full of white teeth. He has one crooked tooth on the bottom which somehow makes him even more endearing. "You'll be surprised."

"The churches picketed our little theater when it showed Fifty Shades of Grey."

"Did you go to see the movie?"

"Yes."

"Were there many others there?"

"It sold out all three screens...at a midnight showing."

He crosses his arms and smirks. "See? Sex sells. People may protest, but they'll be some of the same ones who will sneak in the back door after the sun goes down. I warn you, I will require long days from you in the beginning. It takes a lot to set up a new business. I'd like to get the store organized and stocked so we can open in the next two weeks."

I still don't think it'll last, but I need a job. Even if this place goes under in a few months, it'll hold me over until I can find something else.

"Are you offering me the job, Mr. Lawson?"

His lips jump into a grin again. "Do you think you can learn to call me Wyatt?"

"I'll do my best."

"Then yes, I'm offering you the job. Why don't we return to the back and we'll discuss salary and benefits."

"Are you going to keep the front windows blacked out?" I ask, curious.

"Yes, but not with the paper. We'll hang black and red curtains. In bigger cities, we'd have a display window set up, but in these smaller towns, more people will shop if they can't be seen from the outside. After all, if they're discovered by someone they know while shopping, that person must be here for the same reason and can't judge."

The rear door opens and an older gentleman walks in. I recognize him from the maintenance department of Crunchy Time. He's going to flip his shit when he realizes what the job is. I feel bad, though. It reminds me I'm not the only one out of work and struggling.

"Good afternoon, Sir," Wyatt calls to him. "If you'll have a seat, I'll speak to you when I'm finished with this young lady."

Wyatt leads me to a tiny back office where he gives me the details of the position. He gestures to a chair and sits in the one next to it, so close his leg keeps brushing mine. My eyes widen and my heart rate increases when he tells me the salary, and not just because he's sitting so close.

It's not going to make me rich, but it's considerably more than I made in the factory, more than any of the factories in town, as a matter of fact. If this lasts, I'll be able to get a decent car, maybe even move to a better apartment eventually.

"Like I said, this is a salaried managerial position. It will require long hours until we're up and operational, then you'll work the typical forty hours per week. If you do well enough in training, you'll be the general manager and be responsible for making the schedules for the hourly employees, so you'll eventually be able to set your own hours."

This job is just too good to be true. "Training?" I ask.

"I'll be training you over the next few weeks. I know you said you've never held a managerial position before, but I'm sure you'll do fine. Do you have any questions for me?"

Can we start my training today? Maybe by showing me the proper way to bend over a desk?

"When do I start?"

"Be here tomorrow at noon. We'll start organizing the store. I'm looking for two more salespeople if you know someone trustworthy. They have to be able to pass a criminal background check."

My thoughts go to Jani, one of my friends from Crunchy Time who also just moved into Orchid Apartments. She takes care of her mother and needs a job. I know she wouldn't balk at selling sex toys.

"Actually, I do know someone. She worked at the factory with me. Her name is January. I could call her."

Standing up, he says, "Great. Tell her to come in today if she can and I'll interview her."

His hand swallows mine in a handshake and a shiver races across my skin as his fingers slide across my palm when our hands part. "Welcome to the team, Ms. West. I'll see you at noon tomorrow."

"I'll be here. And please, call me Cass."

"Cass," he agrees with a smile. Damn, what his voice does to my name. Not to mention my lady parts.

We walk back to the rear storeroom where the older man waits. Before I leave, I give him a smile. "Orchid Apartments is looking for another maintenance man. One of ours retired last week. In case this isn't what you're looking for."

"Thank you," he tells me, and I give him a nod before stepping out the door into the pouring rain.

Jani is going to be so excited when I tell her I've found her a job less than twenty-four hours after we were let go. Running to my car, I jump in and text her.

Me: Big news. May have found us both a job. Can you meet me at Carl's?

My phone beeps almost instantly.

Jani: Now?
Me: Yep
Jani: On my way.

Carl's Diner is nearly empty when I arrive since it's between the breakfast and lunch rush. Jani waves at me from the back booth.

"Wow, you must've put that pedal down to beat me here," I observe, sliding into the booth.

"My mother is driving me batshit. I can't watch one more

minute of reality TV. Now, what's the job you were talking about?"

The waitress approaches and takes our order, so I wait until she walks away to ask, "So, how do you feel about vibrators?"

Jani nearly spits out her drink. "Well, I guess I'd have to say I'm pro vibe. Is this one of those deals where you throw sex toy parties at home? Because I'm not going to be able to spend money to get started."

"No, but you would be selling sex toys. The old dollar store is going to re-open as an adult store."

"Get the hell out of here!" She sits back in her seat. "It won't last no time. These self-righteous bitches wouldn't know a dildo if it slapped them in the face."

I try to swallow a laugh when I see our waitress, a lady who looks at least sixty, standing behind Jani. "Honey, if you're getting slapped in the face with it, you ain't using it right," she says, placing our food on the table.

"Sorry," Jani mumbles, mortified.

"Don't be. Just tell me about this store. Are you talking about the building across from the feed store?"

"That's the one."

"Well, don't that beat all? Be nice not to have to mail order. Are they hiring?"

"They're still looking for a couple of sales people, last I heard. He's holding open interviews until four today."

"Perfect. I get off at two."

Jani and I burst into giggles when she walks away. "I put in a good word for you. Wyatt is expecting you today. Just know I call dibs on this one."

"You're calling him by his first name. Did you blow him to get the job?"

"No!" I throw my napkin at her.

"But you would have," she teases.

"For free."

"Seriously? That hot?"

"Just wait until you see him."

Jani and I finish lunch, and she promises to call me to let

me know how the interview goes.

The rain has slowed to a drizzle when I park in front of my apartment. The clothes are gone from the front yard, at least. I'm unlocking my door when I'm struck on the head by an acorn.

"Keep it up, you fuzzy little bastard and I'll turn you into a hat!" I yell up at the branches above my head. I'm actually shouting at the psycho squirrel hiding in the branches. I swear it's a sadist. No matter where you stand under the tree, it throws nuts down at your head.

"Cass, you all right?" Jason asks, stepping around the corner. Jason is one of our three maintenance men. Well, two now that Bob retired. Both of them are about as sharp as a mashed potato. Of course, I'm cursing at a squirrel, so who am I to judge?

"Fine, Jason, thanks."

"Yup." He walks away, sloshing through the mud and water as if it isn't there.

I'm so relieved to have found a job, even if it may not last long. I decide to spend the rest of the day catching up on my reading and television since the little neighborhood bonfire has been postponed because of the rain. After all, I have a long day of organizing butt plugs ahead of me tomorrow.

Chapter Two

The apartment is pitch dark and silent when something pulls me from sleep. Sitting up in bed, I glance at the clock. Four a.m. Hmm, maybe I was dreaming. A slight clicking noise sounds from the living room. I've always been a light sleeper so that must be what woke me, but I have no idea what it is. I've lived here long enough to know the normal nighttime sounds of the water heater banging, the furnace kicking on, the air in the pipes.

Without turning on a light, I creep into the living room. I've locked the front door, but as I'm staring at it, the handle begins to turn. It stops, then turns again, back and forth.

What the hell? Ice drips down my spine, and I feel like I'm in one of those cheesy horror movies where the girl always does something stupid like opening the door or calling out "Who's there?"

As quietly as I can, I creep to the door and peer out the peephole. All I can see is a dark figure, definitely a man, standing on my step. There's no way I'm turning on the porch light to get a better look. Instead, I run and grab my phone.

The nine-one-one operator answers quickly. "Please send the police to 207 Violet Circle. A man is trying to get in my apartment."

"Are your doors and windows locked?"

Shit. Are my windows locked? Cold fear washes over me as

I try to remember. "The doors are. I think the windows are."

I'm standing in the hall when I see the back door handle turn. Same as the front. Back and forth a few times before it stops. "He's at my back door now."

"A car is less than a minute away. Stay on the phone with me."

I can hear him walking around the outside of my apartment, back to the front. I feel safer when I know where he is, so I return to the living room after blindly grabbing for a knife I left on the counter.

I hear the pop of the seal on the living room window as he gets it open. "Get the fuck out of here or I'll cut your balls off!" I scream.

Before he can react, a spotlight illuminates the room and relief floods through me at the sound of the officer's voice.

"Freeze! Get down!"

I rush to the window and look out in time to see an officer tackle the guy as he tries to run.

"Ma'am, ma'am?"

I realize the dispatcher is still trying to talk to me. "Yes, I'm here. The officer tackled him. He's sitting on the ground handcuffed."

"I'm going to let you hang up now. Please stay inside until the officer asks you to come out."

"I will. Thank you."

My mind is at ease, but my body hasn't quite caught up, judging by the way my heart is trying to leap from my chest. I jump when there's a knock on the door, but it's just the officer.

"Can you step outside, please?" he asks.

Wrapping my arms around my middle, I follow him out into the cool night air where a group of guys sit in a pickup truck. Apparently, they're his friends. The guy who scared the shit out of me doesn't appear to be a day over eighteen.

He stares up at me with wide terrified eyes. "She told me to come on in! So I wouldn't wake her mother!"

The officer gives him a stern look and tells him to shut up before turning to me. "Do you know him?"

"No, I've never seen him before, and I sure as hell didn't invite him over. He tried to get in my front and back door. He would've been through the window if you hadn't showed up."

"He claims he spoke with you on a dating app and you told him to come on in so as not to disturb your mother."

"Disturbing my mother would be hard considering she's buried out in Jother Cemetery."

"So you didn't speak to him."

"No."

At this point, the boy looks ready to break into tears. "You did! You gave me your address. 205 Violet Circle!"

"Yeah, well, I'm in 207."

The realization of what he's done crashes over him. "I-I got the wrong apartment. I'm sorry!"

The officer turns to him and starts chewing him out. "You're damn lucky she didn't have a gun or we could be scooping you off of her floor."

After scolding him and his friends, he asks me if I want to press charges. The boy's eyes are pleading with me to have mercy. He may have scared the shit out of me, but it was just a mistake. I don't want to get him locked up for being stupid.

"No, it was a mistake, I guess."

The officer nods and his lips tilt up in a grin. "What were you going to do with that? Butter him to death?"

The knife I grabbed from the counter is still clutched in my hand. A fucking butter knife. "I panicked and grabbed the closest thing," I reply with a giggle.

The officer laughs. "I'm going to search them all before I release them, but you shouldn't have any more problems tonight. Don't hesitate to call if you do."

"Thank you."

I toss the butter knife inside on my coffee table, then turn my porch light on and sit outside to watch while the officer searches the young men. Neal, the single dad from across the street, walks over and joins me.

"Are you okay, Cass? Did something happen?"

"Everything is okay. Some stupid kids got the wrong

apartment. He's going to let them go."

"Not all of them, I guess," Neal points out as another officer arrives. The guy who tried to break in and one of his friends are handcuffed.

The officer hands the other a bag of weed and what looks like a pipe or some other paraphernalia to the arresting officer. "That's on them. I didn't press charges."

Neal stays until they all leave and the sky is starting to lighten. "There are no young women living next door!" I blurt.

"What?"

"He told the cop that a woman told him to come on in so he wouldn't wake her mom. The only woman living next door is Lola, and she's sixty years old and disabled. Her son lives with her."

"Yeah, that quiet kid, what's his name?"

"Jasper."

Yawning, I shake my head. "He said 205. I don't know. I guess it doesn't matter. I doubt they'll be back."

Neal gets to his feet. "Still, you need to lock your windows and doors at night. And if you ever have another problem, you call me, hear?"

"I will. Thanks. I'm going to go back to bed."

"Me too. My daughter will be up early."

"Thanks for checking on me."

"Anytime," he says and walks away.

Wyatt is waiting for me when I arrive at Scarlet Toys for my first shift. Instead of the suit he wore the day before, he's dressed in a polo shirt and a pair of dark slacks. It doesn't matter what he wears, he could be dressed in feety pajamas and a sombrero and any woman would be eager to strip him.

After we get all the tax paperwork out of the way, we head to the sales floor to start unpacking the boxes. Wyatt pulls a pink, slinky, baby doll nightie from a box and tosses it to me.

"Where should I put it?" I ask.

"It's your uniform."

Shocked, I'm not even sure what to say. There's no fucking way I'm wearing this in public. After a few seconds, his deep laughter fills the room. "Relax, I'm kidding. You should see your face."

Tossing the nightie aside, I mumble, "You are a sexual harassment suit waiting to happen."

His gaze lands on me and one side of his mouth lifts in a sexy, crooked grin. "I'm a pretty good judge of who can take a joke."

"Remember that when I get revenge."

Laughing, he scoots a box over to me and hands me a printed layout of the store and where the items are to be displayed. I'm happy to know he isn't one of the stuffy, asshole bosses I usually get stuck with. It'll be nice to have a relaxed, fun work environment. And having his sexy ass to look at and drool over is a definite plus as well.

The back door opens and we're joined by Jani and by the older lady who was working at the diner yesterday. He didn't waste any time hiring help.

"Good, everyone's here," he says, getting to his feet and brushing the cardboard dust from his pants. "This is Cassidy West," he says, gesturing to me. "She's the general manager so you'll be working under her once we open."

"And who will she be...under?" Jani asks with a mischievous smile.

Ignoring her obvious innuendo, Wyatt smiles. "I'm the owner, so she'll bring any problems or concerns to me. I understand you and Cassidy know each other, and this is Martha."

Martha gives us a quick wave as he continues, "The last of our little team will be joining us soon, when his church lets out."

I don't know if it's the mention that the last employee is male or that he's coming from church to work at a sex toy store that makes me laugh, but it appears to be contagious as Jani and Martha follow suit.

"Okay, Cass, you can get started, and Jani and Martha,

18

come with me."

After studying the diagram, I decide to start with the wall of vibrators. I drag over a few boxes and locate a step stool so I can reach the top hooks.

Good god, I never realized there were so many kinds of vibrators. Aside from the normal rubber, metal, and plastic, there are a ton of novelty designs.

I can't help but snort at the sight of some of them as I hang the rows of packages. Who in the world would want a Squido? In case you haven't had the pleasure of discovering this little gem, it's a rubber, white, squid shaped dildo, complete with tentacles.

That may be a bit strange, but the whale penis dildo is just plain scary looking. It's more like a stiff plastic spike. Ouch.

I've filled up a couple of rows when Wyatt, Jani, and Martha return. The older man I told about our apartment's maintenance position follows them in. I expected he'd run the second he found out what the business was. I guess there are more open-minded people in town than I thought.

"You can help Cass on the vibrator wall," Wyatt directs as Martha begins arranging lingerie on racks and Jani starts unloading DVD's on the other side of the room.

"Hi, I'm Clarence," the man introduces himself with a warm smile. He looks like he's in his fifties with salt and pepper hair and a short, graying beard.

"Cass," I reply, shaking his hand. I give him the printout that Wyatt gave me, and he nods, getting to work beside me.

Wyatt is moving a ladder around the room, messing with wires under the ceiling tiles. An hour passes in companionable silence as we all focus on the work. I'm sliding a dolphin shaped vibe on the rack when I feel a tap on my leg and look down into bright eyes.

"Sorry, I need to get in here for a moment," Wyatt says.

He could get in whatever he wants. Shit, I'm even willing to try anal and I've always avoided that.

"Sure." I move my step stool aside so he can put the ladder beside it.

He climbs up and starts messing with the wiring, and I

return to stocking just a foot or so below him, which gives me a great view of his ass, right by my face.

I can't resist looking back at Jani, who grins and holds up her hands, squeezing an invisible set of ass cheeks in the air. Martha also notices, and my giggles escape when she bends over and pretends to slap her ass. This poor guy is being ogled by his employees, except for Clarence, who is focused on stocking an inflatable cushion with a dildo attached in the center.

I turn back to my work, but not for long. Wyatt's foot slides and he slips down a rung, his hand instinctively going to my shoulder to brace himself. It keeps him from falling, but my stool tips and I fall flat on my back into a box of vibrators. And not the soft, rubbery ones.

"I'm so sorry!" he exclaims, jumping from the ladder and rushing to me. Clarence does the same. I'm okay, but the breath has been knocked out of me, so all I can make is a pitiful braying noise like a donkey. So attractive.

Wyatt grabs my hands and lifts my arms above my head. His voice is calm and reassuring. "You're okay. Don't fight it. Just let it come back."

I'm finally able to get a gasp of air and the next breath is easier. If you've never had the wind knocked from you before, I don't recommend it.

"I'm okay," I assure them. "But something hard is sticking me in the back."

They help me out of the smashed box and Clarence grabs the object that was poking me. "Good thing it hit your back," he jokes, holding up a large plastic ear of corn, complete with individual kernels. "You could've been impaled on a cornbrator."

"Who the hell wants to be fucked by an ear of corn?" I complain.

"Gives a whole new meaning to the term cornhole," Martha laughs.

"Wait until we get to the dino dicks," Wyatt replies, still looking concerned. "Are you sure you aren't hurt?"

"I'm fine, really." I'm sure I'll end up with a few bruises, but it's no big deal.

Wyatt sighs and runs a hand through his dark, wavy hair. "I could use a coffee. Let's take a break."

Martha volunteers to run to the coffee shop down the road, and Wyatt hands her a credit card to get everyone a drink.

The day goes by faster than I expect and at eight o'clock, Wyatt sends Martha, Jani, and Clarence home. It appears they'll be working from noon until eight while we pull longer hours.

Jani winks at me on her way out the door and calls, "Don't do anything I've already done!"

Thankfully, Wyatt is out of earshot. I have to admit, I'm a little nervous about being left alone with a man who will definitely feature in my dreams and fantasies whether I want him to or not.

He's my boss, and I need this job so I can't sleep with him. At least that's what I tell myself. Besides, the guy is pretty far out of my league. I mean, I'm no uggo, but he's gorgeous and successful. He probably has some beauty queen girlfriend somewhere.

It doesn't matter anyway since he spends the rest of the shift doing paperwork in the back while I put away stock. We finally call it a night around ten and Wyatt insists on walking me to my car. It's a sweet gesture, but the thought makes me laugh. If he only knew what neighborhood I live in and what I dealt with last night.

I'm dead tired when I get home. I'm not used to working long hours and my back is sore from my fall. After a long, hot bath, my bed is screaming my name. I have to be up early to get my hair trimmed before work so it's definitely time to call it a night. First, I check to make sure all my windows and doors are locked since I don't want a repeat of the night before, although I don't think it's likely. I saw the terror on those boys' faces.

"Well, you know the word is getting around about it," Ms. Larkin says in a faux whisper, like the whole beauty shop can't hear her.

I really hate coming here, but it's the only decent place in town that doesn't leave my hair looking like it's been chewed off by goats. It's always so damn gossipy. I pretty much block everything out, but her next words draw my attention.

"Those boys were going to show him what happens when you try that sick stuff here, but they got the wrong house and ended up getting picked up for weed. Can you imagine? They didn't even investigate!"

"What were they going to do?" another lady asks as she waits with a head full of foils.

"Kick his perverted ass up and down the street! Imagine, pretending to be a woman then luring in men so they find you naked! What did he expect to happen?"

"Oh Lord, how did they find out it was a man and not a woman?"

Ms. Larkin purses her lips, clearly pleased by her captive audience. "Minnie's boy fell for it. He answered some ad and traded messages with the guy. He told him he was a lonely woman looking for some fun, even posted a fake picture. Told him to climb through the back window so he wouldn't wake his mother. Well, he fell for it and when he showed up and climbed in, a young guy was waiting for him, naked as the day he was born!"

The ladies all gasp. I can't believe what I'm hearing as all the dots are being connected. They're talking about my neighbor, Jasper. That's why the dude was trying to get in my place. They intended to drag him out and jump him.

I don't care that Jasper is gay, but I don't need him running a damn ad, then telling people to climb in the window when people are getting the wrong apartment. And I have to agree with the gossiping old biddy on one thing; what did he expect would happen when the guy arrives to find the opposite of what he's looking for?

This is not good. I have no idea what to do about it, though. Do I confront Jasper, let him know I inadvertently saved his ass? That if they hadn't gotten the wrong apartment, he'd have been beaten to a pulp? I have to at least make sure he isn't still running the ad. Our apartments are connected. It wouldn't be hard for a guy to get the wrong window again.

"What do you think?" Sara, my stylist, asks, handing me a mirror so I can see the back.

"Looks great. Thank you." I pay her and head straight back home.

After arguing with myself for a few minutes, I march next door and knock on the door. Jasper's little red car is parked in its spot, so I know he's home, but he doesn't answer.

"Fine," I grumble to myself. I tried to do it the respectful way, but now I'm pissed.

I grab a piece of paper and write a note.

Jasper,

I tried knocking as I'm sure you know, but you won't answer so you leave me with this option. Please take down whatever ad you're running or at least tell the guys to knock on your door, not come on in or climb through a window. I'm sure you saw what happened last night, but in case you aren't aware, those boys were here to jump you for misleading them on the state of your genitalia. Instead, they tried to get through my window. So knock that shit off before someone gets hurt.

Cassidy

I close the note in his screen door before hopping in my car and heading to work. Now that he knows how close he came to getting jumped, I doubt I'll have any more problems. Seriously, though, it seems like all the weird stuff happens to me.

The next week is uneventful both at home and at work. We get the store squared away quicker than anticipated and Wyatt shows us his appreciation in the form of pizza. Friday evening, Jani, Martha, and Clarence are hanging the last few signs and displays while I work on the first week's schedule. It's not that difficult. Jani, Martha, and Clarence have written down what hours they'd prefer and none are too limiting. The only gap I notice is during the late night hours, and since I'd prefer to keep the late shift, I'm happy about it.

Jani is open to any shift, and Martha would prefer to work early or midday. Like me, Clarence would rather sleep in and close, except on Saturday nights when he has church the next morning. After a few minutes of shuffling things around I've managed to give everyone what they want and provide sufficient hours. As the GM, I don't have to clock in or out. I just have to be here whenever I'm needed to keep things running smoothly.

Wyatt enters with two huge pizzas. His face brightens with a smile that never fails to make me picture him naked, and he announces, "I thought we could all use a little reward for a job well done."

A general cheer goes up and a few minutes later we're all seated on the carpeted floor eating pizza. "Is everyone ready for our grand opening tomorrow?"

"I'm ready to see if anyone will actually show up," Martha replies, voicing the same fear I have.

We have a sign that reads "Parking in Rear" posted out front. If that isn't the funniest shit to post in front of an adult shop, then I don't know what is. Anyway, the idea is to allow customers to park where they can't be seen from the street in the hopes that they'll be more likely to come in and shop.

"The grand opening ad will run in tomorrow morning's paper in town and in some of the surrounding towns as well. People will show up. Curiosity will draw them in," Wyatt assures us.

Jani crosses her legs and leans back on her palms. "Speaking of curiosity, boss, I have a few questions."

Oh no. There is no telling what will come out of this woman's mouth. I called dibs, but she also knows I have no intention of fucking around with my boss no matter how much I want to lick him. Or wrap my hands around that hair and pull it while he...

"Go on," Wyatt replies. Damn, there I go again, just fantasizing about him in front of everyone.

"You don't wear a ring so I assume you aren't married. Girlfriend?"

Yep. Straight to the point.

Wyatt laughs and shakes his head. "Not currently, no. I work a lot which forces me to move a lot."

"Awesome answer."

The corner of his mouth twitches as he regards her. "I also don't get involved with employees."

"Ugh!" Jani falls to her back and lets out a dramatic moan. "Why must I need this job?"

Everyone laughs, and Martha swats her on the leg. "Don't you have a man?"

"Not one I wouldn't totally throw out on his ass." She sits up. "Are you married, Martha?"

"For thirty years," she announces proudly before turning to me. "Cass, any beau's at the moment?"

"Nope, can't say there are. I did have a guy try to get in my window last week, but sadly, he had the wrong house." I'm no virgin, but the truth is I've never had a real relationship. "Clarence?" I ask, shifting the focus to him.

"Not married, but I have a boyfriend."

There's one I didn't see coming.

He turns to Wyatt and asks a question I had wondered about but didn't want to ask. "By the way, do we get some kind of employee discount?"

We all burst into laughter, and Martha snorts. "Right? No fair paying full price for your butt plugs."

"Martha!" I swat her arm. "Just because he's gay doesn't mean he uses butt plugs."

"What?" She shrugs. "What's wrong with butt plugs? I have three!"

After we hear that hilarious—if not slightly disturbing—information, Wyatt speaks up. "Yes, you get a twenty percent discount on everything."

Jani laughs and gets to her feet. "There you go, Martha. You can stock up."

"Don't think I won't, missy."

The absurdity of someone who uses the word missy and can also talk butt plugs and vibrators cracks me up.

We spend the next few minutes getting to know each other a little better before Wyatt calls it a night. "We've got a long, exciting day tomorrow."

Chapter Three

It's a completely normal morning until I show up at work. I listen to the radio as I get ready and some of my neighbors wave at me as I drive away. Nothing prepares me for the sight I see when I turn the corner onto the street where Scarlet Toys is located. The bright red sign has been uncovered and it looks fantastic, but it barely catches my eye because my attention is focused on the virtual traffic jam and the crowd around the store.

What the hell? Surely, we aren't going to be that busy. I mean, I remember when the supercenter first opened and people were lined around the block like they were waiting to get in a concert, but for sex toys?

I turn on the smaller road that leads behind the building and am relieved to find it empty. When I pull into the back parking lot, I realize what's going on. It isn't customers or curious onlookers gathered around the building. They're protesters. A lot of protesters.

Wow, if the Fifty Shades movie irked them, this really lit the fuse on these bitches' tampons. I notice it's mostly women, but there are a few men mixed in, carrying signs and shouting slogans.

As soon as I get out of my car and head for the door, I'm spotted and they practically sprint toward me. "How can you go in there? Don't you know they're selling hellfire and damnation?

What would your mother think?"

All of this is being screamed in my face and one of the women gets close enough to step on my foot.

That's it.

"My mother would tell you you'd better get the fuck out of my face before Jesus watches me whoop your ass!"

The woman's mouth forms a perfect O and she steps back. An arm wraps around me from behind just as I'm being surrounded by screaming protesters, and I turn to shove the person off before I hear Wyatt's voice. "It's me. Let's get inside."

Martha pulls in right beside me and jumps out, completely fearless. As they start to shout at her as well, she gives it right back. "Mabel, I see you. Get off your high horse. Maybe if you'd gone for a vibrator instead of your gardener, Mike wouldn't have left you and you'd have something better to do with your time!"

A snort of laughter escapes me and I grab her arm, pulling her inside with us where Jani and Clarence are waiting.

"Holy shit!" I exclaim, as the chants fade away behind the heavy door.

Wyatt's concerned gaze sweeps over me. "Are you okay?"

"Yeah, I'm fine. She just stepped on my foot." I shake my head and a tiny grin sneaks onto my face. "I hate to say I told you so..."

I love his laugh. It's deep and genuine, and he throws his head back with abandon. Sexy as hell. "I didn't quite expect this level of blowback, but it'll pass. It's not the first time I've had to deal with dissent from the locals. The police are on their way now to move them back and make sure any potential customers can get inside safely."

Clarence glances around the store. "Is there anything you need done in the meantime?" Wyatt brought us all in because he expected a lot of customers, but also so we could all get on-the-job training the first day.

"There are a couple of boxes in the back that were delivered this morning. Mostly lube and novelty condoms. You can get those put away."

Wyatt crooks a finger at me. "Come with me a moment,

Cass. I've finally got the uniforms in."

"Yeah, I fell for that one before," I grumble, following him. He stops in the hallway, just out of sight and earshot of the others. Surprised, I step back, my back pressing against the wall. His fingers close on a stray lock of hair on my cheek and tuck it behind my ear as his gaze locks with mine. "Are you okay? I should have had security here to walk you inside, but I didn't expect this level of opposition."

I open my mouth and a squeak comes out. Seriously, I squeak like a damn mouse whose tail has been stepped on. We've spent at least ten hours a day together for over a week, but this is the closest I've been to him. He smells fantastic, some kind of musk mixed with soap and his natural scent. It takes all my restraint to resist sniffing him like a psycho.

"You smell amazing!" I blurt out.

Yep. My ability to talk returns and that's the genius statement that leaps from my mouth.

His lips raise in a smirk and I can't tell if he's pleased, trying not to laugh at me, or planning how to fire the weirdo who can't answer a simple question. "I'm sorry! I didn't mean that."

His smirk widens to a full blown smile.

"I mean, I did. You do smell. Good, I mean. Not bad. If you were stinky, I wouldn't say anything."

For fuck's sake, Cass, *shut up.*

His eyes heat as they sweep over my body, and I feel all the moisture in my mouth dry up. He's never looked at me like that before. At least I don't think he has. I'm probably reading too much into an expression. Just because he looks like he's just seen a supermodel naked and spread eagle doesn't mean anything.

"Do I make you nervous?" he asks, shifting his body closer to mine.

Only when you look at me like I'm dinner. "No," I lie, tugging my earlobe.

"Good. We're going to be here late tonight. I'd like to take you out for dinner after we close."

I can't think of anything to say. "Why?" Is he asking me out? Is it a reward like the pizza?

"Do I need a reason to take a beautiful woman out to dinner?"

"You…you told Jani you don't date employees."

His finger slips under my chin and he lifts my head until we're eye to eye. My heart races when his gaze drops to my lips before returning to my eyes. For a second, I'm sure he's going to kiss me and I don't think I've ever wanted anything as badly as I want to know how those thick lips feel.

"I'm not interested in Jani," he replies before stepping back.

I release my breath. What the hell was that? As soon as he got close to me I felt an attraction I've never felt before, like some powerful force was drawing us together. And his reply. He isn't interested in Jani, but he is interested in me?

Oh, this could go so, so wrong. If there's one thing those few seconds showed me it's that I completely lose my mind in this man's presence. If he had kissed me, I'd have had him naked with no regard to our surroundings. He's my boss. And I know that fucking your boss is never a good idea no matter how sexy he is smiling at me from the office doorway. Shit. I'm just standing here staring at him again.

Composing myself, I follow him inside. It's a tiny space, made smaller by the large box on the desk that he starts digging through. He whips out a white polo shirt with Scarlet Toys embroidered on the upper left side and tosses it to me. "You'd better not pull some booty shorts out of there next," I tease, trying to act like he didn't faze me.

He shakes his head. "As tempting as that is, you can wear whatever you like with the polo."

"Assless chaps and a leotard it is."

Chuckling, he grabs shirts for the rest of the staff. "Are you always a smart-ass?"

I shrug. "Just comes naturally to me."

"Wyatt!" Martha calls from the front of the store.

"Dinner tonight," he says, and rushes off to see what's going on.

Two officers stand on the sales floor, chatting with Clarence. I recognize the cop who showed up to catch my late night visitor last week, and he gives me a nod.

"Wyatt Lawson?" the officer asks.

Wyatt sticks out his hand and they shake. "Yes, sir. I'm sorry to have to call you out here. I've contacted a security company that can start this afternoon."

"We can't keep them from protesting, but we can make them stay on the sidewalk and grassy area. We've cleared the parking lot and entrance, and we'll keep a couple of guys posted until your security shows up."

"Thank you. I really appreciate the help."

"In the meantime, it'd be best for you to continue as if they aren't present. Retaliation is just going to rile them up."

Wyatt blinks. "I have no intention to retaliate."

The officer suppresses a grin, and his partner chuckles. "Sir, pulling in, I saw a bare ass in your front window, followed by a giant bobbing dildo. I understand the impulse, but it's really not helpful."

Wyatt glances around the room where Jani, Martha, and Clarence all give him a "who me?" look and sighs. "It won't happen again."

The officers head toward the door. "Just give us a call if you have any more problems."

Wyatt hands out the polo shirts. "Okay, no more screwing with the protesters. They're like stray dogs. You feed them and they'll keep coming back. Jani, you and Cass can work the counter while Martha and Clarence finish stocking."

The chime above the door dings, and two young women walk in. They look a few years older than me. "Hi, welcome to Scarlet Toys. Please let me know if there's anything I can assist you with," Wyatt greets.

The women take one look at him and suddenly require extensive assistance. "Well, my friend is getting married and we're in charge of the bachelorette party. Of course, we never come to places like this." She glances at her friend, and they giggle like grade schoolers. "Maybe you could show us a few things."

"Of course." Wyatt leads them away and they follow, all eyes on his ass. I can't blame them. It is a fine ass.

"They're making a move on your man," Jani teases as Martha and Clarence join us at the counter.

"What the hell are you on about now?" I sigh.

"Yeah, like we can't see the way he watches you. All those late nights alone with him." She leans against the counter. "Fess' up. And I want details. How big are we talking? Banana? Cucumber? Oh no, it's not a skinny little carrot, is it?"

"I have not seen his vegetable, you crazy woman."

"Well, he sure wants to show it to you," Martha laughs.

My knee bumps a shelf of batteries, knocking a few to the floor. "He hasn't said or done anything inappropriate. It's not like that," I argue, picking up the batteries.

Clarence scoffs.

"Ugh, not you too," I grumble.

"Cass, I know when a guy is interested and trust me, he wants you."

"Maybe he's got his eye on you. You never know," I tease.

"I know I'd drag him home to Harvey in a second, but he's made his choice," Clarence chuckles.

"Is Harvey your boyfriend or is that what you named your penis?" Jani teases.

Clarence shakes his head. "My boyfriend. Who the hell would call a penis Harvey?"

"I knew a guy who called his Mr. Galifianakis," Jani replies.

I chose the wrong moment to take a drink of water and it sprays out of my nose as I try not to choke to death.

"What?" Jani asks, thumping me on the back. "It was bearded."

The chime dings, and two more customers enter, followed by three more. Maybe Wyatt was right after all. People do seem willing to walk past the protesters to check us out.

Customers stream in throughout the day with a few lulls. All in all, things go really well, despite the rough start to the morning. Wyatt lets Jani, Martha, and Clarence leave about an hour before closing, and Jani gives me a told-you-so look as security escorts them to their cars.

The last of the protesters have gone when Wyatt locks up

and we leave the building. We aren't open on Sundays, so everyone has the day off tomorrow before beginning our normal schedule on Monday.

Wyatt hasn't mentioned dinner again, so I'm headed toward my car when he steps in front of me. "Is that your way of turning down my dinner invitation?" he asks, feigning a hurt look.

"I thought you might be tired and ready to get home. You know, you aren't quite as young as me," I tease.

"Ten years is a drop in the bucket. You'll see."

I cover my mouth like I'm shocked. "Ten years! You're thirty-one? Do you remember when this was all farmland?"

I'm spun around with my back against the door of his car before I can laugh at my own joke. "Ten years of experience goes a long way." His hands clamp on my hips and his breath heats my neck as he leans in and murmurs, "Tell me you aren't interested and I'll leave you alone, Cassidy. But if you don't speak up now, I'm going to kiss you until neither of us can breathe."

I can't breathe now.

Fuck it, who needs oxygen anyway?

I slide my hand behind his neck, and our lips come together in a soft, slow kiss. The world around me fades away as his hands travel to cup my face and tilt it until he has me where he wants me, his lips brushing lightly over mine again.

The tip of his tongue strokes my lips, and I groan as it dips inside. My hand travels up his nape into his soft hair. I know two things instantly. I never want to stop kissing this man. And this job can go straight to hell if it becomes an obstacle. I'll gladly clean toilets with a toothbrush at an Indian restaurant if it means I get this kind of reward at the end of the day.

We deepen the kiss, exploring one another's mouths, and his arms wrap around my back, pulling me against his body. The feel of his hard chest against my breasts makes my nipples perk up. It isn't the only thing that's standing at attention, though.

Judging by the size of the hard-on poking me in the stomach, he doesn't think he's out of my league. His lower lip is plump, and I can't resist sucking on it before we break apart, drawing a soft hum from him that seems to travel straight to my core.

I may only be twenty-one, but I can't imagine another first kiss that will ever beat this one.

Our town pretty much rolls up the sidewalks after eight p.m. so we end up at a Mexican restaurant in the nearest city, about thirty minutes away.

Wyatt opens the door to the restaurant, placing a hand on my back and guiding me inside. My mom would've loved this guy. He's got what she always described as hoity toity manners. Like having a guy open your car door or walk you to your door is a privilege of the upper class. And why is it always about doors? Whenever women describe a gentleman, they mention he opens doors for them. When did that become the standard?

After we're seated, I order a margarita to try to settle my nerves. It's not every day I'm out with a man who looks like he jumped from the cover of a fitness magazine. "So, um…why did you choose our town to open a store?" I ask, trying to break the ice.

"I'm trying to win a bet…sort of."

"A bet?"

The waitress delivers our food, and I start eating as he explains. "I've worked my way up in my father's company. He plans to retire in a few years, and I'm hoping to take over the company. The only thing we disagreed on was my desire to expand our adult stores outside of large cities. Finally, he made me a deal. Open two stores in two small towns. If I can get at least one of them to survive, then I can take over the company when he retires. If they fail, I'm stuck in my current position."

"So, you have a lot invested in this. That's good to know." I grin at him. "For job security and all."

His expression is serious when he replies, "I won't let it fail."

"So far so good. Protesters are a pain in the ass, but at least people are coming in. I imagine there will be more once the protesters get tired and move onto something else."

"That's what I'm hoping." He sits back in his chair. "So, tell me, are you from Morganville?"

"No, I moved here when I was ten with my mom. She died a few years ago, right after my graduation. I don't have any family left in Missouri, where we came from, so I just found a job and moved into a cheap apartment. I plan to go to college someday, once I figure out what I want to do and save some money."

"You should. You're smart."

"You've seen me stock dildos and run a cash register," I laugh. "It's not exactly rocket science."

I notice the small flecks of black in his amber eyes when he regards me. "No, I've seen you problem solve and serve customers who were shy or embarrassed. You have a way of putting people at ease, and that's something that can't be taught. You should consider going into business classes."

My cheeks heat with a mix of embarrassment and pleasure. I'm not used to compliments. "Is that why you wanted to take me out? You were impressed by my customer service skills?" I tease.

A devilish grin spreads across his face. "Actually, I was hoping to take you home and show you some of my servicing skills."

I'm stunned into silence for a moment before I reply, "And you come off as such a gentleman."

"Only at work, sweetheart."

"I'm not looking for anything serious," I tell him. I'm not really averse to relationships all together, but I'm sure this is what he wants to hear. We come from two different worlds. He's most likely looking for a little fun, someone to hang out with and fuck while he's here. I'm more than willing to have a fling.

"I'll only be in town for a few months, then I'll be returning to Indianapolis."

Wiping my mouth on my napkin, I sit back. "You don't have a secret girlfriend or wife at home, do you?"

His laugh is deep and gravelly. "There's always been this rumor among men that women decide whether or not they'd sleep with a guy in the first ten minutes after they meet. I don't think that's typically true, but with Wyatt, I knew in the first five.

"No, I work too much to maintain a serious relationship." He smiles at me. "And I'm not sleeping with anyone else."

Grinning like my heart isn't beating out *fuck me now* in Morse code, I shrug. "Your place or mine?"

"I'm staying in a hotel, so…"

"My place, then," I tell him. No need to feel like a total whore accompanying him back to his hotel room. "Let's get my car from work and you can follow me back."

It's a silly thought. I've never been the type to sleep around. Hell, I've only been with two guys; my high school boyfriend and a drunken hookup who still texts me occasionally. Neither of them were any good in bed. Something tells me that won't be a problem with Wyatt. I could come just looking at him.

Wyatt pays the check, and we head back to town. It's getting late and the highway is pretty much deserted. "Do you mind?" I ask, reaching for his radio.

"You don't listen to country, do you?" he asks, his adorable crooked tooth showing as he smiles at me.

"God, no. All I listen to is Justin Bieber. Did you know he has his own station now? Nothing but the beebs twenty-four seven." I intended to draw the joke out a bit, but the look of horror on Wyatt's face forces a laugh from me. "I'm just screwing with you." I tune the radio to a rock station, and he reaches over and grabs my knee.

"Think you're funny, don't you?"

Grinning, I roll my window down. "I'm very amused by me."

His grin spreads and he drops his window as well as I crank up the music and start singing along to one of my favorites. I'm weird and impulsive. He may as well learn that about me right now.

Apparently, he's not bothered because he starts belting out the lyrics along with me. His voice is smooth and deep and does nothing to quell the urge I have to fuck him senseless. We spend the rest of the ride back singing and laughing, the warm summer wind blasting across our skin. It's fantastic.

He drops me off at my car, and I hesitate a little before walking away. "My neighborhood is a little...strange. Fair warning in case you see anything crazy."

"I'm sure I can handle it," he laughs.

I lead him back to my apartment complex, and he parks beside me. It's after midnight, but the circle never sleeps. Samantha is ushering a man through her front door and she turns to give me a wave before disappearing inside.

Wyatt joins me and he looks toward the playground across the street where the swings are creaking as two shadows sit on them. "Doesn't the park close at night?" Wyatt asks as I unlock my front door.

"There are hours posted, but no one pays any attention. It's probably a couple of guys from Frat Hell." I continue when he gives me a confused look. "There's a large, four-bedroom apartment on the other end of the circle. It's rented out by a bunch of college kids. It's not really a fraternity, that's just what the rest of us call it. They party a lot."

As soon as I get mine unlocked, the neighbor's door flies open and Dennis comes running out, stark naked. He's holding his hands over his crotch as his belly flops around. A barrage of objects fly out after him and a hiking boot pops him right in the forehead.

"Go run to your diseased whore! And don't forget these! Let her wear the fucking strap-on, you pervert!"

Sure enough, her words are followed by the launch of multiple dildos, flying through the air like pecker confetti, one still attached to a pair of panties meant for a strap-on. Dennis is as red as I've ever seen a human being get as he grabs a pair of pants from the ground and yanks them on.

He glances in my direction and mumbles, "Cass, do you think I could borrow a trash bag?"

"Sure," I reply, fighting back laughter. It's not the situation that's funny, really. Granted, throwing him out naked is a new occurrence, but I'm used to their knock down, drag out fighting. What has me about to burst is the expression on Wyatt's face.

Yeah, I tried to warn him.

"I...do you want me to call the police?" he asks, following me into my living room.

"For what?"

He stares at me like my slinky is kinked. "For the naked man in the yard."

"He's not naked anymore. They fight a lot. Tomorrow, everything will be back to normal. They don't hurt anyone," I tell him, heading to the kitchen and grabbing a trash bag.

He takes it from my hand when I return. "I'll give it to him."

It's cute how he's suddenly so protective, but it's really not necessary. I hear Mallory screeching about crabs when the door opens and a giggle escapes me. Wyatt looks back and smiles, shaking his head.

"Weird neighborhood." I shrug. "You get used to it."

I head to my room to grab something to wear and deposit the clothes on the bathroom counter. After working all day, I need a quick shower. When I peek out the window, I see Wyatt helping Dennis pick up his stuff and put it in the trash bag. The dildoes are no longer in sight.

By the time I shower and dress, Wyatt is sitting on my couch in the living room. His lips part when I enter—gah I'm always looking at his lips—and he looks at me like I'm dressed in lingerie instead of a tee shirt with little cotton shorts. He pulls me down on the couch beside him.

"Mmm...you smell good." His light stubble scratches my neck as he buries his face there. "I can't wait to see how you taste."

A good licking from Wyatt? Fuck. Yes. Sign me up.

"Do you mind if I use your shower?"

"Of course not, there's a robe hanging in the bathroom if you want to wear it."

"I have a change of clothes in the car. I live out of a suitcase, remember?"

There are times I dream about traveling, living a nomadic life, but I think the novelty would wear off quickly. It may not be much, but this place has become my home. It would be depressing to live out of hotels and never feel at home.

Look at me, feeling sorry for someone who could probably buy this whole place. I may be overestimating his wealth, but I've grown so accustomed to being surrounded by people like me, who struggle and live paycheck to paycheck. The fact that he owns two stores and has worked his way to an executive level in his father's company makes him rich in my eyes.

The money doesn't change anything, though. I'm no gold digger. I enjoy being around him. He's easy to talk to and always kind, which is a hard quality to find sometimes. Plus, you know, he looks like he stepped off an underwear ad.

I didn't expect to bring a man home with me when I left for work this morning, but at least my bed has nice, fresh sheets and my room isn't messy. While Wyatt is showering, I connect my phone to my speaker, choose a playlist, and put it on shuffle.

He returns wearing only a pair of sweat pants, his bare chest displaying a light sprinkling of dark hair. I love chest hair. Like, it's probably an unnatural love. While other women expect men to wax or shave everything, I'm fantasizing about running my cheek across those curly hairs.

"If you keep looking at me like that, I can't be held responsible for my actions," he warns, his eyes full of lust as he stalks toward me. I suddenly feel like prey, but I'm only too happy to be devoured.

"Pshh...like I'm so impressed by your carved chest and swollen biceps."

I'm sitting on the edge of the bed when he walks up between my legs and stares down at me. "I've got something much more impressive for you."

His pants are expanding right in front of my face so I have no doubt he's telling the truth. My mouth goes dry and teasing him is the last thought in my head. I want this man naked and on top of me.

I rub my hands up his chest as I stand. He's so damn tall I'm tempted to stand on the bed. Instead, I throw my arms around his neck, and he leans down, bringing his lips to mine. His hands wander underneath my shirt until he's cupping my bare breast while he owns my mouth with his tongue.

Wyatt's kiss is intense and exciting. It steals the world from around me and all that's left is him, the feel of his tongue exploring mine, his fingers caressing my nipples, his hand kneading my ass.

We part long enough for him to pull off my shirt, then our mouths clash together again. His back is warm and smooth, lined with muscles I can't wait to lick, but my hands have a mind of their own when they slide down the back of his pants. I've never felt such a squeezable ass. Even through his clothes, I could tell it was a great ass, but I'm still pleasantly surprised by how round and firm it is.

His fingers hook into the waistband of my shorts and panties, and he removes both with one movement, pausing to let me step out of them. I'm generally happy with my body, even though I'm too skinny and my boobs struggle to reach a B cup, but this is the point where I'd usually become a little self-conscious.

Not this time. When Wyatt gazes down at me, all I see is the lust and appreciation that's mirrored on my own face.

"Such a beautiful body," he murmurs. "Such a shame I'm going to dirty it all up."

If it isn't clear by now, I talk a lot. I babble and say dumb stuff when I'm nervous. What I never do is get tongue tied, but this man has managed to steal my words. There isn't a thought in my head other than I can't wait to be dirtied up.

He smirks, obviously aware he's thrown me off kilter, and yanks off his pants. Of course, he doesn't wear underwear. His cock is every bit as impressive as he claimed. It's perfect really. Long and thick, but not so big I can't take him.

The smirk is knocked off his face when I bend forward and give it a long, slow lick around the head. He grunts and his head falls back for a second before I'm snatched off my feet. "As much as I'd love that, I have other plans for you tonight, babe."

He tosses me on the bed and yanks my legs apart. Standing at the edge of the bed, he stares down at me for a long second, making me feel exposed. "You're blushing," he murmurs, bringing his gaze to mine.

"You're staring at places I can only see with a mirror," I

reply, finding my voice.

"Get used to it. I plan to look at this pussy every chance I get." His fingers brush gently between my legs. "And touch it, and fuck it, but right now, I want a taste."

Soft lips lay kisses up my thighs until he reaches his target. The first brush of his tongue between my folds make me gasp and raise up off the bed. A wicked smile appears on his face as he wraps his arms around my thighs, pulling me down and holding me open to his talented mouth.

Maybe I've only been with guys who didn't know what they were doing or only knew the "lick the alphabet" trick, but I've never been able to come from this before. I had no idea it could be so incredible and overwhelming. Within minutes, I can feel the pressure building.

"Oh fuck. Yes…don't stop. Don't stop," I plead.

I don't know what little move he pulls, but I can't stop from crying out as I'm seized by the sudden, devastating pleasure. The spasms go on and on as he continues to lick and suck. When I finally relax, I realize my hands are buried in his hair, trying to pull it out.

"Sorry," I mumble, scratching at his scalp.

"Don't you dare be sorry."

He gets to his feet and grabs a condom from the pocket of his sweats, still balled up on the floor beside him. Seconds later, he's crawling over me, his huge body looming above me like something right out of one of my Tarzan fantasies. The Alexander Skarsgard Tarzan, of course.

The heat of his solid weight on top of me feels so damn good as he showers both of my breasts with attention. God, his mouth. He has the best mouth. Damn it. I said that out loud.

His eyes delve into mine as he slides inside of me. It takes a few deep breaths before I can acclimate to his size, and he gives me a moment before he starts to move. Pain quickly gives way to pleasure, and I throw my legs around him.

As soon as I start moving with him, he groans and increases his pace.

The man can move.

40

It's unfair, really, for one guy to have everything he does. Money, looks, a fun personality, a big cock, and moves that could win him a stripper award. If that's something that exists. Either way, the man is a damned artist in bed.

He doesn't just slam in and out of me, like the guys I've had before. He moves with purpose, and grace that shouldn't be possible for a man his size. It feels like he's hitting every nerve ending in my entire body every time he presses forward, and when I feel like it can't possibly get any better, he shifts his hips and proves me wrong.

I don't know how long we keep at it. It feels like forever and I never want it to end. Our moans and pants echo around us, overcoming the music as we both near the edge. "Wyatt," I gasp before burying my face in his neck as I'm thrown into an orgasm every bit as strong as the first.

I feel him still, and a growl rumbles his chest as he comes. Seriously, a growl. It's probably the hottest thing I've ever heard.

It's instantly followed by the opposite of that.

My music has continued to play, but I barely heard it and I doubt he did either. Unfortunately, there's no missing the song that's filling the room now.

The theme song to Scooby Doo.

We're lying here, covered in sweat, his cock still inside me, listening to the Scooby Doo theme song. Before I can comment, his body begins to shake with laughter and he looks down at me. "Ruh-roh," he says, and we both fall into hysterics.

He rolls off me and goes to dispose of the condom while I stop the music that has totally killed the moment.

When he returns, he climbs back into my bed and pulls me close. "Do you always fuck to Scooby?" he teases.

"Nah, Flintstones is my jam." Giggling, I lay my cheek on his chest. "I forgot I added a couple of kiddie songs when I was babysitting one of my neighbor's kids."

"Uh-huh. Sure," he teases, tickling the back of my neck. "So, if I look at your phone I won't see a wide selection of cartoon songs? Maybe a little Captain Caveman when you're feeling freaky?"

"Hmm…you do growl like a cave man when you come."

His fingers thread into my hair and he asks, "Do you mind if I stay the night?"

Did I hear that right? I was seconds away from getting up and letting him know I didn't expect him to stay, and he wants to spend the night?

"Of course you can stay, but if you need to go, I understand." I'm trying to give him an out, but apparently, he doesn't want one. The hotel must be lonely.

"I don't have anywhere to be until tomorrow afternoon," he says.

"Good, then I can hear you growl in the morning too."

Rolling over and tucking my body against his, he drops his voice to a deep rumble. "Captain Caaaavemaaan!"

Chapter Four

Wyatt proves his skills again the next morning before we both drag our asses out of bed and shower. It's the first day off either of us has had in a while so neither of us is in any hurry to do anything.

We end up lounging on the couch, eating donuts. "These commercials kill me," I remark with a chuckle as an ad for a prescription drug plays. "There's always a long list of side effects that are ten times worse than the condition they're treating. I mean, did you hear the last one? Uncontrollable flailing of the arms and legs? So, would I turn into one of those inflatable tube men the car lots have out front?"

Wyatt laughs and starts speaking in a deep announcer's voice. "Do you have dry eyes? Just use two drops of Clearitup every night. Side effects may include morning breath, rectal prolapse, back hair, sudden hate for the color yellow, an urge to eat gravy, and loss of sphincter control."

Stretching out, I lay my head in his lap. "Ugh, a craving for gravy and no sphincter control would not be a good combination."

"Zoinks," Wyatt replies, and I slap his arm.

"I'm never going to live that down, am I?"

"Not any time soon."

A teddy bear made of denim falls off the back of the couch

and Wyatt picks it up. "Your bear is suicidal."

Closing my eyes, I snuggle against him. "Maybe because his stitches are crooked. I screwed up when I was sewing his head. It gives him a lot of character though, so I didn't fix it."

"You made this?" he asks.

"Yeah, making plush animals is sort of a hobby." I peek up at him. "What do you like to do when you aren't conquering the world one dirty store at a time?"

His hand is warm in my hair. "I like to fish and ride my jet ski. Play video games."

"I suck at games. I die a few times then get pissed off."

Wyatt chuckles. 'I'd like to see that. I'll bet you're adorable when you rage quit."

"Of course. I'm always adorable."

I can't believe how much fun I have with Wyatt. He's different outside of work, funnier and more relaxed. We hang out until early afternoon, and he kisses me goodbye before he leaves, promising he'll see me at work the next day.

I'm ignoring multiple alarms blaring in my head at the moment. You know, those bitter, hating little voices that want to warn you of impending bad ideas to destroy your fun. So he won't be in town long. I just won't get attached. I'm not the clingy type, anyway. And so what if he's my boss at a job I really need. We're adults. We can be professional at work and naked at home. No problem.

The heat wave has finally broken so I grab a glass of tea and sit out on my step to enjoy a little sunshine. Mallory and Dennis must still be on the outs since he's sitting on a bench at the park across the street, his trash bag full of clothes beside him. Whenever they fight, she usually lets him back in by morning. He really must've screwed up this time. I did hear her scream something about crabs, though. That's not something you just forgive.

I realized a long time ago that you don't need cable television if you live on Violent Circle. We have the outside channel. Twenty-four seven entertainment that's free and includes all the drama you'd usually see on a reality show.

"Hey, Cass," Noble calls, coming to take a seat beside me. "How have you been?"

Noble Bradley lives in the Frat Hell apartment. He's about a year older than me, and cute, but a big partier. He's getting ready to start his last year of college, though, so he must be able to handle it.

"Pretty good."

"I hear you're working at the sex shop." He flips his blond hair off of his forehead and grins at me. "Can I come and get a happy ending?"

"I can recommend a top of the line Pocket Pussy if you're hard up," I offer, chuckling.

"Please," he scoffs. "I get more ass than that park bench." His gaze lands on Dennis. "Guess Mallory threw him out again."

"Looks like it."

Noble produces a joint and offers, "You want some?"

"I'll hit it once or twice." I shrug. I need to do laundry today and if I get stoned early, I'll get nothing accomplished.

Dennis makes his way back across the street while we smoke, and marches past us like he doesn't see us. Or maybe he wants to pretend we can't see him. He starts banging on the door and pleading with Mallory to let him in. When those pleas fall on deaf ears, he starts demanding she give him his car keys.

"You want me gone? Fine! Then let me get my damn keys!" he insists.

"Aw shit," Noble mumbles, covering a grin as the door pops open.

Mallory shakes a keyring in his face. "Are these what you want, huh?" She storms across the yard and down toward the entrance to the apartments. He follows her and even once they're out of sight, their shouts and threats filter back to us.

"See that? That's why I stay single," Noble says, putting out the joint and stashing it in his pocket. "You know the block party is next weekend, right? You coming?"

"Yeah, kind of hard to miss," I reply, and he nods.

Mallory is stalking back up the street, but Dennis isn't behind her. "Mal, you okay?" I ask. "Do you want to come in for a few?"

She pauses to talk to us. "Thanks, but I'm fine."

"Where's Dennis?" Noble asks.

"Looking for his keys in the sewer."

Noble's eyebrows race up his forehead and he snickers.

Swallowing back my amusement, I ask, "You threw his keys in the sewer?"

There's a gleam in her eye when she answers me. "Nope." A keyring hangs off her finger when she holds up her hand and shakes the keys like you would to get a baby's attention.

It takes about two seconds for both Noble and I to lose it. It's mean, but it's just too damn funny. "He-he's down there in the water, looking for keys you never th-threw in?" My laughter keeps interrupting my words.

The circular road we live on dips on one end as it leads out of the apartments. Whenever it rains, the water all flows toward the sewer drain at the complex's entrance. It's a deep drain that gets backed up a lot and usually holds about two to three feet of sludgy, disgusting water. On really hot days, the odor that emanates from it can turn your stomach.

Mallory shrugs. "Trick works on my dog and Dennis ain't no smarter. Teach that bastard to cheat on me." As soon as she disappears into her apartment, Noble looks at me and we both crack up again. It really is too funny.

Noble gets to his feet. As he walks away, he calls out, "We're going to have some spiked watermelons out back during the block party. Come and join us. Bring Jani."

"Okay. Thanks for the buzz."

"Sure thing."

Bring Jani. Noble has been trying to get in Jani's pants forever. She doesn't give him the time of day, but he doesn't give up easily.

It's laundry day so I walk down to Jani's apartment to see if she wants to go with me. There's no chore more boring and mundane than laundry, so we usually go together to quell the boredom.

It's late afternoon, but she answers the door with sleep

mussed hair. "Bitch, were you still asleep?"

"I was up all night," she grumbles, turning on her coffee pot and pulling two cups from the cabinet. "What are you doing out all chipper and shit? I figured you'd barely be able to walk today."

Another thing about living on the circle, nothing is private. Almost half of the apartments face the other half so everyone sees what you're doing. I guarantee most of the neighborhood saw Dennis's naked ass outside last night. You'd think that would've distracted from the fact that I had company.

"Stalker."

"I saw Wyatt helping Dennis pick up his clothes," she laughs.

"You missed the best part. She threw a bunch of vibrators at him and announced that he makes her use a strap-on. Then today she pretended to throw his keys in the sewer, so he's still down there digging for them."

Jani's head whips around and she snorts out a laugh. "You're kidding!"

"Nope."

A steaming coffee cup is set in front of me and she takes a seat across the table with hers. "Wow. Wonder what he did?"

"She was screaming about crabs, so it's a safe bet he cheated."

Jani's jaw drops and we both succumb to laughter. "Well deserved then," she says.

Yeah, we're gossiping. I'm not the type to spread rumors or anything and neither is Jani, but she's my best friend and we do get a laugh out of the chaos that surrounds us.

"What did Wyatt think of all that?"

"He only saw the fight last night." I shrug. "I'm going to invite him to the block party, so if he accepts, I guess it didn't scare him away. Now, get dressed so we can go to the laundromat. These are my last clean pair of panties."

"Panties are not a necessity."

"Not for a trollup like you," I tease, getting to my feet. "Meet you at mine?"

"Give me a half hour."

"Okay, bye hooker face."

"Hope a bird shits on your face, bitch!" she calls out as I leave.

That's my bestie.

Laundromats seem to showcase the oddest people. At least it seems that way whenever I go to our local Suds-N-Rinse. Jani and I go to our usual spot, the back corner, where we claim a couple of washers and the nearby table.

Emily, another tenant from Violent Circle, waves before turning back to one of the customers. She appears to be in some kind of heated debate. By the time we have our clothes loaded and the washers running, a police car pulls up front.

"Looks like we get a show today," Jani remarks, as an officer leads a young guy outside. The guy is ranting and raving about femi-nazis.

Emily approaches us shaking her head. "I swear, it's like a full moon or something. Nothing but crazies today."

"What did he do?" Jani asks.

"Spit on a woman, then told her she'd better get out of those wet clothes." Emily sighs and flops down into a chair.

"What the hell?" Jani exclaims.

"Pickup line of the year," I laugh.

Emily grins. "Like we don't get enough crazy at home. You going to the block party?"

Why does everyone keep asking me that? It's taking place right outside my front door. "Yeah."

Jani bends over and starts separating her colors. "She's bringing our new boss."

"Ooh, the guy from Scarlet Toys? He's fine as hell."

Hopping up to sit on the table, I turn to Jani. "Noble said to make sure I bring you. They'll have watermelon soaked in alcohol."

"Good. I want to celebrate. I dumped Trevor last night."

Trevor is Jani's friend with benefits. At least, that's how she described him. I knew it wouldn't last long, even though they were exclusive. Jani always finds something wrong with them, some reason to break up. She's totally dedicated to avoiding a real relationship.

"You did? What happened?"

Jani plunks in her quarters and turns on the machine. "He refuses to keep a job. I'm not dating a loser who never plans to leave his mother's house."

"Good call," Emily says. "Noble has been watching you forever. Are you ever going to put that boy out of his misery and throw him a little?"

"No way. I need at least a little maturity and Frat Hell is definitely lacking in it. Have you ever heard them discuss their house rules?"

"What are they?" Emily asks.

"I guess there's a list a mile long, but the last one I heard was that any time one of them eats a banana, they have to be on their knees and maintain eye contact with one of the other guys."

Emily and I crack up, and she gets to her feet. "Great, Skid Mark Steve is here, my favorite customer," she grumbles. "Gotta go. See you at the party."

"Ew, why can't the guy do his own wash?" I remark, as my washer buzzes.

"Poor Emily," Jani agrees. "I'd rather sell butt plugs any day."

We finish our laundry and part ways. I spend the rest of the evening hanging out at home, just lounging on the couch. It's been a long week and I'm sure the next one will be too.

Finally, I drag myself to bed, and I'm out almost instantly. A few hours later, I hear a tapping on my window. I know everything is locked up, including the screen, and I'm pretty sure what's going on this time, so I raise the window. I'm face to face with a middle-aged man who says, "Jade?"

"Jade," I grumble. "Could he have picked a trashier name?" Sighing, I give the guy the bad news. "No, I'm not Jade. You have the wrong window. I hate to break it to you, but there's no Jade. The asshole next door is the one you're looking for, but unless you're into cock, I wouldn't bother."

Shocked, he steps back. "Are you serious?"

"No, I always make up elaborate stories when some guy tries to get in my apartment."

"The message said—"

"To climb through the window, I know. Again, you have the wrong window, and my neighbor's a dude. Good night." I jerk the window shut. This shit is ridiculous. Somehow, I don't think the average person deals with stuff like this. Only on Violent Circle.

I don't bother to see if the guy leaves or tries Jasper's window. Instead, I crawl back into bed and manage a few more hours sleep before work.

The week goes about as well as the last one. We still have to be guarded by security since the protesters are still going strong. It doesn't stop customers from streaming in, though, and by the end of the week, I'm starting to think Wyatt is right. Scarlet Toys can outlast the protesters.

Jani leaves first on Friday night, leaving me and Wyatt to close the store. She's barely out the door when I'm pushed against the wall and his tongue is in my mouth.

He kisses me stupid, then steps back and grins. "I've been thinking about doing that for hours."

God, every time I see this man, his beauty hits me like a punch in the face. I've had that gorgeous face between my legs. You'd think I'd be acclimated to seeing it by now, but no.

"I don't think this is proper office behavior," I tease.

"I'm not proper. Come home with me tonight." His hand starts to travel down my shorts, but I grab it.

"Sorry, Mr. Proper, off limits at the moment. Somebody poisoned the water hole."

He steps back and his entire face is a question mark.

"It's shark week? The gauge is in the red?"

"Oh, you're ovary-acting!" he laughs, kissing me on the forehead. "Doesn't mean I don't want you to come home with me.

We'll just watch a movie or something."

I want to. I really do, but we've been spending a lot of time together. This is supposed to be about sex. Just a little fling until he leaves. "Sorry, I just want to go home alone and curl up with a book and enough chocolate to choke an elephant. Do you still want to go to the block party tomorrow?"

"Absolutely, just tell me what time."

"Around three?"

"I'll be there."

The Fourth of July block party last year ended with one of the guys from Frat Hell blowing off the tip of his finger with a firework if that tells you the kind of party I'm anticipating tonight. If Wyatt wasn't scared away by seeing Dennis's naked ass, I imagine he can handle this.

"Well, if it isn't the magical disappearing slut," Jani calls as I step out my front door. She's sitting on Samantha's step, and I can smell the weed they're smoking.

"Starting early?" I walk over to join them.

"Mom is feeling pretty good, so she's spending the holiday at my cousin's house. I'm free." She grins up at me, offering me the joint. "And it's time I got details, so spill it. Tell me that sexy fucker is terrible in bed so I don't have to hate you." Jani hands the joint to Samantha when I shake my head.

"Not going to be able to do it. For once, I found a man whose skills match his body."

Samantha laughs. "That's a rare thing. The last guy I was with who was all muscle and cock had no idea what to do with it."

A sudden bang sounds from the other end of the circle, followed by loud laughter. "It's coming from the duckling's place. Kids are running wild while the older one from next door lights firecrackers," Jani explains.

One of the three bedroom apartments on the end houses a couple with four kids, all under five years old. When they walk them over to the park, they stay in a line like ducklings.

"So, any bet on how early an ambulance will be called this year?" I ask, pulling my phone from my back pocket.

"It'll be a miracle if we make it until dark," Samantha replies.

Wyatt pulls into the parking space in front of my apartment and Jani chuckles. "Look who's slumming it. I can't believe you invited Mr. Hot and Proper. He's going to run away screaming."

With his expensive clothing and high class manners, everyone sees him as a stuffy rich guy, but I know better. "Nah, he can handle a little trashy fun."

Wyatt approaches with a smile on his face, and Samantha murmurs something that sounds like *ride him like a cowgirl*. "Good afternoon, ladies," he says.

"It is now," Jani remarks, her gaze traveling over his body. He's dressed casually, in shorts and a navy tee.

Ignoring her, he wraps an arm around my waist and drops a quick kiss on my lips. "Am I early?"

"Nope. They're already grilling burgers in the playground. The street will be full within an hour."

"Would you like a drink?" Samantha asks, beating me to it.

"I was about to offer the same thing," Wyatt replies. "I have a cooler full of beer in my trunk."

"Wyatt, this is my neighbor, Samantha," I tell him, and he reaches out his hand.

She shakes it, practically licking her lips at the sight of him. I can't even blame her. That was my first reaction too. "Nice to meet you," she replies, offering him the joint in her hand.

"No thanks."

"You don't smoke?" Jani asks.

"Occasionally, but I'll pass for now, thanks."

Linking my arm through his, I pull him away from the two women I know are imagining dirty things in their heads. "Come on. Let's take a walk. I'll introduce you to the other crazies."

The whole neighborhood is out, and more people are pulling in and parking beside the playground every minute. It may be the residents who throw this party every year, but plenty of other friends and relatives show up.

Two large grills are smoking away at one end of the playground, manned by a couple of older guys I've said hello to, but don't really know. There's a massive game of tag going on that seems to include adults as well as kids.

Coolers are scattered about, with signs that offer the contents to whoever wants a drink or a snack.

"Cass! Over here! We've got cornhole!"

"Not sure I'd be announcing that," Wyatt mumbles with a grin.

"You have no idea what cornhole is, do you?" I ask, pulling him toward the back of the apartment building.

"No, and I'm a little afraid to ask."

Noble stands by a large, folding table which holds a massive watermelon. One of the other Frat Hell guys, Denton, begins cutting it up, and Noble hands me a chunk. "Tell me if it's strong enough."

It's hot out and the sweet, cold juice tastes like heaven. If heaven was dipped in vodka. Wincing, I swallow. "Yeah, definitely strong enough."

Wyatt accepts a chunk as well and he and Noble start talking about some video game stuff while I wander over to talk to some of the other neighbors gathered around the picnic table.

"Careful, hun," Neal cautions. "There's a bunch of poison ivy around that tree. My girl has already got into it. Had to send her home to wash off."

"You can't wash off poison ivy."

"Yeah, I know, but it couldn't hurt."

Actually, it's likely to spread the oil around that causes the rash, but I'm not going to argue. It's too late anyway.

At that moment, Trey, another guy who lives in Frat Hell appears wearing a pink baby bib and carrying a yellow toddler's sippy cup.

"What the hell?" Wyatt laughs as Trey, Noble, and Denton join us.

"This is Wyatt," Noble says to Trey. "He's here with Cass.

Wyatt, this is Trey, who spilled his beer in the middle of the living room rug and now has to drink like a toddler."

Judging by the cheesy grin on his face, Trey is drunk already. "I told you, it was Kenny! He kicked it over!"

A head pops out of the window. "Lies! All lies!"

"I demand a trial by combat!" Trey announces, yanking off the bib.

Wyatt, Neal, and I step back out of the way, and lean against the fence to see what these crazy guys are going to do next. Kenny stalks out the back door carrying two sets of huge, inflatable boxing gloves.

Stepping back, Noble announces, "A trial by combat has been declared!"

They both put on the gloves and proceed to beat the crap out of each other until Trey finally ends up on the ground and taps out. Laughing, Neal, Wyatt and I leave them still arguing over who has to wear the bib and drink their beer from a sippy cup.

A few hours later, the party is in full swing. Jani sits beside me on a picnic table and we watch a bunch of the guys play basketball. Wyatt has no trouble fitting right in with my friends and neighbors. He may have been raised rich, but he definitely isn't stuck up about it.

"Your man can slum it pretty good," Jani says, handing me a Jello shot.

Wyatt reaches over his head and pulls off his shirt, wiping his sweaty face with it before tossing it aside. I'm so fixated on watching him, I barely hear Jani sigh.

"Oh, he's definitely going in the rub club."

"Jani!"

"What? Like I'm the only one who saw that in slow motion? He may be yours, but he has a starring lineup in my fantasies now."

"What about Noble?" I tease. As if he hears his name, Noble winks at Jani, and gets rewarded by a body check that puts him on the ground.

"Pass. Wyatt, though. Fuck, Cass, you hit the sexy jackpot."

Taking another drink of my margarita, I roll my eyes at

her. "You can stop drooling over him now."

"Relax, you get to actually get him naked. He's just a figure in my dirty imagination."

I can't blame her. I can barely take my eyes off of him myself. His face lights up with a charming smile when he looks my direction, and I suddenly feel like a fumbling high school girl with a crush again. His chest is covered in a light sheen of sweat, and as he lifts his arms to shoot the ball, the muscles in his back flex and tighten. My mouth damn near waters at the sight of him bending over to scoop up the ball when the game is finished.

"Aw, look how hot he is. You know what he needs?" Jani says. "A go on the slip and slide."

My drink attempts to escape through my nose when I laugh. Yeah, of course she wants to see him all wet and soapy and...why am I not going along with this?

"Agreed," I murmur as he approaches me.

Slinging his shirt over his shoulder, he sits beside me and puts his arm around my neck. "You're all sweaty," I squeal, and he chuckles, pulling me into his lap.

"You like it. I saw you over here watching me."

"Maybe I just thought a tall guy would have some game." I shrug.

"You are a terrible liar."

When I look up at him, his lips are inches away from mine and I can't help myself. He doesn't seem to mind the PDA though, so I grab his lips with mine. He tastes like the cherry sports drink he's been guzzling, and I can't get enough of him. A second before I can suggest we go back to my place so I can blow him like a party horn, Jani speaks up.

"So, we were just heading to the slip and slide, Wyatt. You up for it?"

He grins down at me. "Cass?"

"It's not the kind of slip and slide I had in mind right now, but sure, why not?" I nip his ear with my teeth. "Then we go back to my place."

The slip and slide is a homemade monstrosity created by the guys from Frat Hell. Huge sheets of plastic line the small hill at the playground and stretch across the park, ending in an inflatable kiddie pool. Since water alone wasn't a fast enough ride, they've added dish soap so the whole thing is a mass of bubbles.

A small crowd is gathered around it, and there are as many adults taking a turn as there are kids.

"Age before beauty," I tell him, handing him an innertube.

"That smart mouth. I'm going to have to find a way to keep it busy."

The thought sends a flush across my skin, and I wonder if he can tell that I want nothing more than to take him back to my apartment and demonstrate what my mouth can do. "One turn, and you're coming home with me," I inform him in a voice just low enough so the others can't hear.

Grinning, he steps back and announces loudly. "Just let me have one turn, Cass! Then I promise I'll take you home and let you touch me."

The neighbors all crack up, and I flip him off.

"If you aren't willing, I'll gladly fall on that grenade!" Samantha shouts.

It's a good thing I'm not a jealous person. Wyatt grabs the innertube and dives down the hill, and I do the same right behind him. Cool, soapy water sprays over me as I barrel down the strip of plastic and into the kiddie pool where I crash into Wyatt. His body is slick beneath my hands when he plants a kiss on my lips.

"I have so much fun with you, Cass." It's a simple statement, but the sincerity in his voice grabs my heart. After all the pickup lines and bullshit I've heard in my life, just hearing he likes to be with me and knowing he means it makes me feel warm and happy.

"I like being with you too. You're not nearly as stuffy as I thought you'd be when we met."

Laughing, we climb out of the pool. "It was the suit, wasn't it?"

"Mostly, and the manners. I love both of those things though, so don't you dare change."

"Nope," he agrees, linking his arm around my waist as we walk back. "I can wear the shit out of a suit."

"I also enjoy your modesty and your lack of competitiveness."

"Of course you do," he agrees. "I'm the most modest."

We're drawn away from our silly conversation by shouts coming from across the street. Two men I've never seen are screaming at one another and a crowd is starting to gather around them.

"Do you know them?" Wyatt asks.

"No, they don't live here."

Both men are obviously drunk, and no one intervenes when the most ridiculous attempt at a fistfight kicks off.

One man, wearing a white tank and cargo shorts, shoves the other. The momentum sends both of them to the ground and we watch as they take a long minute to get back to their feet. The other man is clad in only a pair of basketball shorts that are hanging too low.

"Was my beer, you chuckle fuck!" white tank guy slurs.

Jani rolls her eyes. "They're fighting over a beer? There are coolers full of free drinks everywhere."

"Hush, we'll miss the show," Noble says, stepping up behind her and resting his hands on her shoulders. I'm a little surprised she doesn't shrug him off or kick him in the balls or something, but she just focuses on the fight in front of us. Which only gets funnier and more pathetic.

At least four punches have been thrown, but none connect, and they spend the majority of the time circling each other. The guy in the basketball shorts keeps closing one eye, trying to see straight. It must work because he finally manages to punch tank top in the mouth.

Tank top shoves him down, wobbles on his feet, then grabs a political sign stuck in the yard to steady himself. Too bad the sign is made of poster board. It gives way under his weight and he goes down again.

Pissed off about the punch, the other man gets to his feet and grabs the sign, yanking it out of the yard and coming at tank top with it. That would be funny enough, I mean, what the hell does he think he's going to do with a flimsy sign? It isn't until tank top screeches like a fifties woman who just saw a mouse, and tries to run away, that the crowd really erupts into laughter.

"All right. I think that's enough." Two officers step up from behind us. I didn't even notice them pull in. Tank top spews a line of curses and insults a mile long while he's being cuffed, but the other guy isn't going to go down so easily. At least he doesn't think so.

He pivots and tries to run, but the second officer just sticks out a foot and down he goes. He flops hard onto the grass, sliding a bit, which pulls down his shorts, baring his ass to the crowd, that roars with laughter.

"Police brutal, bolice prutality, police brutality!" He yells as the officer cuffs him, stands him up, and pulls up his shorts.

The crowd cheers as the two men are charged with public intoxication and lead away.

The sun is just beginning to set and it won't be long until the big fireworks show. "Come on," I urge Wyatt. "I want to get dried off before the fireworks."

"After I get you wet, you mean."

"Too late."

"You're killing me, woman."

"Too bad I'm still closed for business. But I might have a little something for you."

After a very satisfying shower, we head back outside for the fireworks show. The local radio station nearby puts on a big show that's set to music, and it's visible from our little circle. Afterwards, the shit really hits the fan when everyone else sets their own fireworks off.

Blankets are spread across part of the park and we find an empty place to sit. Wyatt sits behind me while I curl up between his legs. His arms slide around me, pulling me back against his chest. He's warm and I've never been so comfortable. Someone tunes their radio to the correct station and we watch the flowers bloom in the sky as Bruce Springsteen's Born in the USA blares around us.

It strikes me how amazing today has been. Wyatt fit in with my crazy neighbors and friends, and I'm learning more and more about him. It never feels awkward or forced. It's like I can be myself with him, and I think he feels the same.

As the fireworks dwindle, his phone rings and he excuses himself to answer it. His expression when he returns makes it clear something is going on. "I have to take off in a few minutes."

He hands me a set of keys. "I need to leave town to deal with some issues at my other store. It'll only be for a day or two, but the store is yours until I return."

What?

"You want me to run it while you're gone?"

A smile breaks across his face. "That's what I hired you for. You have the number to the security firm if you have any additional trouble, and they'll be there as usual to keep things under control. You can always call me if you need help with something."

I'm not worried about the store. I just don't want him to leave. The thought flashes in front of me like a big, red warning sign, and I swear I hear a loud buzzer in my head accompanying it. Abort! Abort! Feelings are being caught!

"Sure, no problem." I shrug. "I hope everything's okay at your other store."

We walk back to my place together where he kisses me goodbye and promises, "I'll call you tomorrow."

It feels strange to be the one opening Scarlet Toys. This is how it'll be when Wyatt leaves town for good. I hadn't really thought of the responsibility I'll have when that day comes.

"Hey Boss Lady," Clarence says, approaching me as I unlock the door. "Wyatt messaged to let everyone know you're running things."

"He'll be back in a couple of days."

"There seems to be fewer protesters today," he remarks, clocking in.

"I noticed. It's still early, though."

"Do you want me on the register?"

I've never been in a manager's position before and it seems weird to give orders. I suppose I'll get used to it. "Yeah, I'll set up the new display."

Everything is quiet for the first hour or so until one of the security guys asks me to walk outside with him. The protest is back in full swing, but that isn't what he wants to show me. He walks me to my car, and I freeze. My passenger side windows are shattered. The front one is completely gone and the back is barely hanging in the frame.

"What the fuck?" I exclaim.

"I'm sorry. I've already called the police and messaged Mr. Lawson. He wanted to know if there were any problems."

Of course, it was one of the self-righteous assholes who did it, but I don't know how. "How did they get past your guys to get to my car?"

He sighs. "They didn't." He reaches inside the car and produces a pellet. "They shot the windows with a pellet gun. One of my guys got the plate number, so I'm sure they'll catch them. I'm sorry. This happened on my watch."

I look up at the large man who seems genuinely stricken. "It's not your fault. You can't predict crazy and these people are definitely one banana short of a fruit salad."

My phone starts ringing and I'm not surprised to see Wyatt's name appear. "Cassidy, are you okay?" Wyatt asks, not even giving me a chance to say hello.

"It was just my car windows. The store is fine."

"I was asking about you, not the store."

"I'm fine. The cops are on their way and your security got the plate number."

"Good, I'm arranging for a garage to pick up your car and a rental will be delivered before the end of the day."

"My insurance doesn't cover a rental." It doesn't cover vandalism either, but I'm not telling him that. "I'll bum a ride from Jani until I get it fixed."

"This happened because you work for me. I'm fixing it. End of. If you want to close up for the rest of the day—"

"No," I interrupt. "We're fine, really. You put me in charge so you need to trust me to handle this."

There's a pause before I hear him chuckle. "I obviously chose well. Call me if anything new comes up."

"I will."

The cops show up and take my statement, but they're more interested in talking to the security guys since they witnessed what happened, so I head back inside.

The sight of cop cars in the parking lot doesn't deter customers, if anything, it seems to bring them in as everyone wants to ask what happened and pass around the gossip. I'm actually glad when we hit a lull in the afternoon.

The bell on the door dings, and in walks some familiar faces. "Hey Cass," Noble calls. "Jani working today?"

"Not until four."

"Cool."

Noble is accompanied by a few of the other Frat Hell guys and they all browse around, laughing and teasing each other. "Do people still buy porn on DVD? Don't they know Pornhub exists?" Denton laughs.

"You'd be surprised. They sell pretty well," I reply.

Denton is the only one to purchase anything, and the other guys laugh when he places a giant box of condoms plus our biggest bottle of lube on the counter.

"Trying to keep your Fleshlight clean?" Noble taunts.

"Nope, I like to leave my own special sauce in there so I know you assholes won't touch it. These are for the house."

"Community condoms aren't a bad idea, but community lube? No way," Kenny says.

"Like you ever get laid," Denton scoffs.

"I'm not the one resorting to plastic pussies."

They keep up the back and forth until Noble asks why the cops were here earlier. After I explain, he steps back. "Fuckers! Don't worry, we've got your back."

It's sweet, but it's also not what Wyatt would want.

"We have the cops dealing with it, but thanks."

Noble peeks out the front curtain at the yelling, marching

crowd. "They don't give up, do they?"

Clarence laughs. "Not with the sin of masturbation running rampant. At least that's what they like to yell."

"Fucking ridiculous," Noble grumbles.

Clarence regards me after they leave and the store is empty. "They're going to do something stupid."

"Probably," I sigh. This manager shit might be harder than I thought.

True to his word, my car is picked up and a rental left in its place before the end of my shift. I end up staying until close because I don't want to leave Jani and Martha alone after what happened. By the time I get home, I'm exhausted. Twelve hour shifts suck.

Wyatt calls and promises to be back by the following night. We chat for a few minutes before I turn in for the night.

Tomorrow has to be better.

Chapter Five

The protesters seem to be emboldened by the events of the day before. There are more than usual, yelling and carrying their signs, and security has to keep them away from the building.

This shit is really getting old.

Clarence is opening with me again and we spend the first hour arranging a new shipment of lingerie. Jani shows up early and bursts inside, laughing too hard to talk.

"Cass! Come on!" she struggles, yanking open the front curtains. "You have to see this!"

My first thought is that I told those idiots not to retaliate. It's quickly replaced by a feeling of pure bliss as I burst into laughter. The Frat Hell guys are out front and they've brought friends. A lot of friends.

The whole group of boys are shirtless and most have some kind of saying written on their chests and backs. They also carry signs like the protesters, but with vastly different slogans.

They've just joined in the protest like they belong there and tears run down my face from laughing, not just at their antics, but at the expressions of the protesters.

I spot Noble, his chest smeared with red paint and *Masturbation is Murder. Every sperm counts!* scrawled on his back. He's marching beside a guy holding a *Smut Peddlers Burn in Hell* sign, and the guy doesn't look pleased. Maybe because Noble's sign is drawing far more attention.

Hugs not Butt Plugs! is printed in solid black letters and is apparently the slogan of the day since Noble and the Frat Hell guys are chanting it, drowning out the others.

Denton is a few feet behind him, chanting and carrying a sign that reads, *Dildos are a DilDON'T.*

"Oh my god!" Jani exclaims. "What the hell is that?"

A person jumps out of a car in a T-rex costume. A sign dangles from one of the little arms that reads, *Fappy the anti-masturbation dino says hands off!*

It's a damn mad house out there. The original protesters are going strong, only stopping to give dirty looks to the newcomers who are mocking them. The guys' chant of *Hugs not butt plugs* is growing louder by the second. I need to do something.

Carl, one of the security guys, meets me just outside the door. "We can't stop anyone from protesting," he explains, chuckling. "As long as no one is getting hurt, we have to let it continue. Maybe they'll actually run some of them off."

A scream of "Real men don't fuck plastic cooter!" rings out. Carl's gaze meets mine and we both lose control. My sides ache from laughing.

"I know who the ringleader is." I point out Noble. "Can you ask him to come in and talk to me?"

As fun as this is, and no matter how much they deserve it, we aren't going to get customers with all this going on. I need to put an end to it.

Noble enters with a huge smile on his face. "Fappy the dino has a crowd twerking with him! You're missing it!"

Crossing my arms, I try to suppress a grin. "Didn't I tell you not to antagonize them?"

A smirk raises his lips. "Antagonize? We're just joining in. Masturbation does a lot of damage, you know."

"To your palms, maybe," I laugh. "Look, Noble, I appreciate the effort, really, but I'm in charge for the next few days and I need to keep this shit under control."

"Fine, I'll call off the guys."

Noble follows me back to the sales floor, and I peek out the front window where a few outraged shrieks reach my ears. Fappy the Dino is now marching with a giant super soaker and spraying random protesters. One of them—a middle aged man—shoves him and knocks him onto his back where he lies, legs cycling in the air as he tries to get up.

Noble smiles at my giggles. "Those tiny hands are a bitch. I'd better go. Don't come outside for a bit. That's not just water in the super soaker."

Oh shit.

"What's in it?" I ask, pulling the curtains shut again.

"The poison ivy leaves from my backyard may have found their way into a bucket of water and soaked overnight."

Jani approaches from behind us, a horrified expression on her face. "You didn't!"

Noble shrugs. "I wasn't sure it would work, but Denton poured the water into the guns this morning and dripped a bit on his wrist. He had a rash within an hour."

Jani gazes at Noble with what I could swear is awe and admiration. Apparently, she's impressed. "Damn, I'm gonna start calling you Ruth," she says, shaking her head. "Cause you're ruthless."

"You can scream whatever name you like when we're in bed," Noble replies, and Jani scoffs.

"All right. Go call off your friends before things get any uglier," I order. Noble nods and heads for the door, turning back when I call, "Hey, Noble! Thanks."

Grinning, he nods again and disappears outside.

I can't resist watching out the window as Fappy proceeds to mess with one of the older male protestors. Sneaking up behind the guy, he grabs the sides of his *No Smut!* tee shirt and starts to hump him. The man spins around and shoves him, dropping his sign, and Fappy snatches it up, chasing him with the stick end, as if he's going to plant it somewhere really uncomfortable.

Noble grabs Fappy's tail and holds him back, yelling something at him. Fappy drops the sign and lowers his head, plodding back to the van they came in. The whole thing is complete chaos, and I see a few people filming with their phones, so I have a feeling I'll be seeing this scene again.

A few minutes later, the crowd is gone, other than the original protesters. I can't help but watch from the front window while more and more of them start scratching at themselves. Within an hour, there are only a few people left and all of them have bright, angry welts on their skin.

Customers have come in pretty regularly throughout the day, despite the turmoil surrounding the building, and I'm happy I'll at least be able to give Wyatt a good sales report, even though everything else hasn't exactly gone to plan.

It's late afternoon, and we've hit a bit of a lull when an older man charges through the door and demands, "Who was in that dinosaur costume?"

"Excuse me?" Jani says, putting on her fake, customer service voice.

The man has a poison ivy rash on both of his arms, and by the way he's scratching, I'm willing to bet there's more under his shirt. "What he did was assault! Everyone who got sprayed has a rash! Who knows what he had in that squirt gun!"

Clarence approaches and pretends to study the man's arm. "It's poison ivy, or maybe poison oak. Either way, you need to wash it and get some cream or it'll keep spreading."

"Assault!" the man shouts again.

Carl steps in the back door. I nod toward the guy, and Carl approaches him. "You need to leave the premises," he warns.

The man jerks away from him. "I'm not going anywhere! Look what they've done to me!" He sticks out his arm and gestures towards us.

"They haven't left the store all day thanks to your little group. If you'd like to lodge a complaint, I suggest you contact the authorities. Right now, you need to leave or I'll remove you."

Carl is not a little guy, and the man must hear the truth in his voice because he huffs and stalks toward the door. "I'm calling the police! I know you know who was in that dinosaur suit!"

After he slams out the door, I turn to Carl. "Thanks for coming to the rescue."

"That's my job." He grins and drops his voice. "Any idea

who the t-rex was?"

"No, but he has my thanks."

"Crazy protesters, a dancing t-rex who sprays poison ivy water on them, young guys chanting about butt plugs. This may be the most entertaining assignment I've ever had," he says with a chuckle.

I stay until closing time again with Jani and Martha, but there are no more incidents. When we all leave, there isn't a protester in sight. I assume they're home taking oatmeal baths.

Karma can be magnificent, even when it comes in the form of a Frat Hell guy.

By the time I get home and shower, Wyatt is texting me.

Wyatt: I'll be back in town in a few hours. Would it be okay if I spent the night?
Me: As long as you realize this is a total booty call.
Wyatt: I can live with that.
Me: I'll probably be asleep. Door is unlocked.
Wyatt: See you soon.

After the last two days, I'm exhausted, and I barely notice when Wyatt climbs in bed with me a few hours later. I snuggle into him and fall right back to sleep.

Wyatt's phone blares, piercing through the three a.m. silence, and I groan as he flips on the lamp and picks it up.

"Yeah?"

I can only hear his side of the conversation, but it doesn't sound good. He sits up, and the sheet falls to his waist. "When? Is it out? No, no one should be inside. Yeah, I'm on my way."

He's on his feet in seconds, jerking on his clothes. "Wyatt? What's wrong?"

"Scarlet Toys is on fire."

His words take a second to sink in, but as soon as my tired brain catches up, I leap out of bed and jerk on a pair of shorts and a tee. Silence wraps itself around us as we hurry out to his car and head toward the building we've spent so much time working on.

The smell of smoke fills the air before we even get close, but the sight of the building with flames licking out of the front window is something I'll never forget. Red lights flash across the darkened buildings and storefronts nearby, and a piercing siren dies off as another firetruck pulls into the lot.

A selfish thought strikes me. I'm probably going to lose my job and Wyatt in one night. The store is a bust, so why would he stay? The sharp ache I feel from that realization tells me it might be for the best. I wasn't supposed to catch feelings for him.

An officer approaches us as soon as we get out of the car, and I recognize him from the time we had to call them on opening day. "Mr. Lawson," the officer says, nodding at Wyatt.

"Any idea how it started?" Wyatt asks, remarkably calm for someone watching his business turning to ash.

"Not yet. Do you have anything flammable or potentially explosive inside? We've heard a few pops."

Wyatt shakes his head. "No."

"Um…" I interject. "It was probably the pressurized cans of flavored whip cream and body paint."

The officer suppresses a grin as he nods and heads over to tell the firefighters the likely culprit. "Wyatt, I'm so sorry," I tell him, sliding my hand into his.

His lips press together as he looks down at me. "This won't stop me."

"You think someone set it on fire?"

"Look." He points to the windows. More than one is broken, and not just near the fire. Even the slim window on the back door is busted out. "That isn't accidental."

"Fucking protesters."

"Most likely. I have insurance. I'll rebuild and upgrade with a sprinkler system and better security." A satisfied grin spreads across his face as he gestures to the light poles surrounding us. Each bears a camera, pointed at different sides of the building. "The assholes who did this are busted and they don't even know it."

"When did you install those?"

"Last week. Once I realized the protests weren't going to die off like usual, I expected some vandalism. Not to this extent, though." His chest rises on a deep sigh. "We have to start over."

Guilt seizes me. How much of this is my fault? Wyatt left town for two days and everything went to hell. Rule number one was don't antagonize the protesters, and I let it happen.

"I'm sorry. I tried to keep everything under control, but…"

"Hey." Wyatt slides his palm against my cheek. "This isn't your fault."

"We had some trouble earlier. Noble and his buddies were antagonizing the protesters. They sprayed them with poison ivy."

He steps back and blinks. "How the hell do you spray someone with poison ivy?"

"Soak it overnight in a bucket of water, then put the water in a squirt gun."

I expect him to sigh or curse or something, so I'm completely taken off guard when he bursts out laughing. "That's fucking genius. If I ever need a revenge scheme, I know who to go to. Did it work?"

"Yeah, a good amount of them were scratching and rashy by the end of the day."

Wyatt chuckles. "I'm kind of sorry I missed it."

"Jani has some video." Yeah, I'll let him see Fappy the dino for himself. No way I'm trying to explain that.

"Still, that has nothing to do with the fire. If it's arson like we expect, I'm sure they would've done it anyway. They want us gone."

"Maybe this isn't the best town for your business," I tell him. The words taste bad in my mouth. I don't want the protesters to win. I like my job. I like my coworkers. I like *Wyatt*. I'm not ready to let any of that go.

His eyes blaze as they clash with mine. "I don't give up, sweetheart. So don't you dare."

"How long do you think? Before we'll be open again?" I'll have to go to the temp service to find a job in the interim if it's going to be more than a couple of weeks.

"I don't know until we know whether it's a total loss or not. It may be better to just tear it down and build again. The place was pretty old. If we have to do that, I'm guessing two months or so. If we can repair this structure, maybe a month if we're lucky."

Shit.

As if he's reading my mind, he adds, "I'll keep you, Jani, Clarence, and Martha on the payroll until we reopen. You've all done great, and I don't want to lose good employees."

My jaw drops as I step back. "You're going to pay us when we aren't working? Aren't you going to lose money?"

He shrugs. "Not enough to make a difference to me. But I know it will to your friends. Plus, I don't want to have to retrain and hire new people if they quit and go onto something else because they have to."

Damn it, he's such a nice guy. I was sure those didn't exist anymore.

Firefighters shatter the front window and continue to douse the flames, which are starting to dwindle.

A fireman approaches us. "We've got it under control. We'll have to watch for hot spots for a while, though, so you won't be able to get in and examine the damage until tonight. You'll want to get in touch with your insurance company."

Wyatt thanks them and then asks me, "Where is the best place to go for donuts?"

Either this guy is truly unflappable, or he hides his emotions really well. He should be beyond pissed, the way I am, but he's thinking about breakfast.

"Foster's Bakery. Down town." I glance at my phone to see it's just past five a.m. "They just opened."

He hooks an arm around my neck and we walk to his car. "Let's go."

The lady working the counter at the donut shop looks half asleep as she boxes up four dozen donuts and takes Wyatt's money. "Hungry?" I tease.

"I figured the fireman and officers might be." He shrugs and picks up the boxes.

"What?" he asks after we return to the car. I might've been staring at him again, waiting on him to spontaneously sprout wings or shining armor.

"Are you always so perfect? It's kind of annoying."

His laughter fills the car. "I'm far from perfect. I have more than most so it's not like it's a real sacrifice to give to others."

My phone blares to life in my pocket. Who the hell is calling before six in the morning?

"What the hell is going on?" Jani demands as soon as I answer.

"Scarlet Toys is on fire."

"No shit! Damn it! Was it the protesters?"

"We're assuming."

Wyatt parks in front of Scarlet Toys, which is now smoldering and smoking. He gets out of the car to take the donuts to the first responders while I talk to Jani.

"I guess we're job hunting again. Fuck. I'd rather shit in my hands and clap," she moans.

"Actually, Wyatt said he's going to continue paying us while he rebuilds. He doesn't want anyone to quit."

The information must stun her into silence because it's a few seconds before she replies, "You're kidding."

"Nope, dead serious."

"You better blow that man until the top of his head pops off."

"I'll take that into consideration," I laugh. "I've got to go. I'll talk to you later."

Wyatt walks up and hands me a napkin with a donut tucked inside before leaning against his car and taking a bite of his.

The sun is starting to come up, illuminating the scene in front of us. Scorched dildos, lingerie, and random sex toys lay scattered across the lot. Most are melted and misshapen, the rubber and plastic bubbled up.

"It looks like the inventory is a total loss, but not the building. It'll take the inspectors and insurance adjusters a week or so to get everything worked out. There's not much I can do here in the meantime, so I'm going to spend a few days back in Indianapolis," Wyatt tells me.

"Is this going to screw things up between you and your father?"

"No, he'll rub it in a bit, since this is the reason he won't open stores in small towns, but he knows I won't give up." He flashes me that devastating smile. "It's not in my nature."

"I talked to Jani. She knows what happened. Would you like me to call Martha and Clarence?"

Wyatt nods. "If you wouldn't mind. I have a bunch of calls to make before we get ready to leave."

Wait, what?

"We?"

He grins at me. "Did I forget to mention you're coming with me?"

"You must have. Is there anything else I'm doing that you forgot to mention?"

He tilts his head back and scratches his chin. "Let's see. You're going to Indy with me, we're going to hang out and relax, and have lots of dirty sex."

Grabbing his waistband, I pull him toward me. "Anything else I should know?"

He shrugs. "Road head is a given."

"Not sure I could drive with you doing that, but yes, I'd like to go with you. Since you asked so nicely." I stand on my toes and plant a soft kiss on his lips. His gaze darkens a little when I look him in the eye and ask, "Are you okay?"

His chest rises and falls on a deep sigh. "I'm pissed."

"Good. So am I."

"And I want to take you home and nail you to the bed."

"After you make your phone calls," I promise, and smack him on the ass. "I'll call the others."

"Tell them I'll put their checks in the mail weekly and be in touch when we're ready to re-open."

Wyatt's place in Indianapolis really opens my eyes to how different we are. I expected a big house, but the fancy, down town penthouse outdoes anything I anticipated. He has his own private elevator that empties into a foyer half the size of my apartment.

"We'll just drop off our bags, then head over to meet with my father."

My head jerks up. "You want me to go with you? To meet your father?"

"Unless you'd rather not. I'd like to introduce him to the manager who can handle anything," he replies with a grin.

I don't know whether to be relieved or disappointed. There's definitely a bit of both emotions running through me as I take a deep breath. For a second, I thought he was introducing me to his father, like a girlfriend or someone important to him. It makes sense he would want to show him one of his new hires. I really need to stop reading too much into this trip.

Wyatt shows me around the penthouse. His living room is a bachelor's dream with a large sectional couch wrapped around a coffee table. A massive television hangs from the wall and multiple gaming systems rest on a shelf underneath.

"You're a total gamer nerd, aren't you?"

"I'm a tech nerd," he corrects, leading me into the kitchen.

He isn't kidding. His kitchen is full of bright, shiny appliances that would look completely at home in a futuristic movie. The refrigerator has a damn touchscreen on the front. "Wow, do you like to cook or is a robot chef going to pop out of a cabinet and start making dinner?"

"Nah, I save the robots for the bedroom."

"As long as it's a male robot. I don't like vagina, metal or otherwise."

Grabbing me around the waist, he pulls me against him and the smile on his face makes me want to strip him. "You have a smart comeback for everything, don't you?"

"It's a gift." I shrug, trying to conceal the response he always seems to elicit from me.

He drops a kiss on my lips and steps back. "Make yourself at home. I've got to get some paperwork together and then we'll go."

"Sure."

Make myself at home? This place is so upscale and pristine,

I'm afraid to touch anything. I feel like a kid in a curio shop where one wrong move could destroy everything. I wander into the living room and take a seat on a couch. I can't help but run my hands over the material. It's so soft it's like petting a blow dried baby duck.

I assumed Wyatt didn't exactly do without anything, but sitting in his penthouse, surrounded by all this splendor I've never even come into contact with before, I realize he's much better off than I thought. It's a good thing our little fling is temporary because I can't imagine I could ever fit into his world.

I glance down at my clothes. I'm just wearing jeans and a tee shirt, my usual go to outfit, but I suddenly feel like a poor urchin drug in off the street.

Wyatt pops into the room juggling a briefcase and a few file folders. "Shit," he murmurs as he drops one and the papers scatter across the floor.

"Come on Lawson, get it together," I tease, and pick up a sheet that landed near me.

My jaw drops and I feel my heart speed up at the sight of the company letterhead.

It takes me a moment to find my voice. "Cavenite Entertainment? I—your company is Cavenite Entertainment?"

Cavenite is a household name. They not only own and operate adult entertainment stores, but also own multiple production companies, both in television and music. They created one of the first and most popular streaming services for movies and television, and that's just the tip of the iceberg. They have their hands in so many industries, they're often spoken of in the same breath as Disney or Amazon.

The heirs to the Cavenite fortune—Vince and Wyatt Cavenite—have graced the covers of magazines since they were children. How did I not realize before who he is?

Looking up at him, I utter, "You're Wyatt Cavenite. Not Lawson."

A cautious expression steals across his face. "Lawson is my middle name."

"What—why didn't you tell me?"

With a sigh, he pulls me down to sit beside him on the couch. God, his father is a billionaire. The couch might actually be made from baby ducks.

"Because I wanted to be successful without using my father's name. It opens doors for me that I'd rather pry open myself. And because of the way people treat me, like I'm a different species because my family has money." The corner of his lip tucks in and he gazes at me. "Because of the look on your face right now."

Damn. He's right. "Pfft, like I'm so impressed by your fancy shmancy stuff."

A small grin cracks his lips.

"I have to know one thing though. And I want to know the truth." He bites his lip, waiting for me to continue. "What is this couch made of? Because I don't think I can hang out with someone who murders baby ducks."

His face blanks for a few seconds before he breaks into laughter. "What the hell are you talking about?"

My hand travels across the creamy soft material. "It's the softest thing I've ever felt."

"So it must be made of baby ducks?"

"Oh no. It's bunnies isn't it?"

Cracking up again, he pulls me to my feet. "I have no idea what my couch is made from. This place belonged to my brother before me, and he hired a decorator. I'm rarely here. I prefer my cabin on Monroe Lake. In fact, after I finish what needs done here, I was thinking we'd head down there."

"You have a lake house?"

"Yeah, I'm not a big fan of living in the city. Would you like to go? We can swim and go fishing or just lie around and relax. In between marathon sex sessions of course. If you'd rather stay here—"

"You had me at marathon sex," I interrupt, holding up my hand.

"All right then. Let's go meet my father, then we'll spend the night here and leave in the morning."

Following him back to the elevator, I glance down at my

clothing again. Once we're inside and headed down to the parking garage, I can't help but ask, "I—I'm not exactly dressed to visit a multibillion dollar company. Your father is going to think you drug me in off the street."

Wyatt faces me and places his hands on my shoulders. His eyes lock onto mine. "No, he's not like that. There's nothing wrong with what you're wearing. The only thing he's going to wonder is how I got such a beautiful woman to put up with me."

My hand travels to wrap around his neck. "You are completely full of shit," I tell him, punctuating my words with a long kiss that makes him groan.

"Are you calling me a liar?" I don't have a chance to reply before he's kissing me, his hand kneading my ass.

"Yep. I'm sure women are throwing themselves at your feet." I bring my lips to his neck and tug on the hair at his nape.

"Not for the right reasons."

He steps forward, making me back up against the wall of the elevator. "Are we arguing?" I ask as he grips my ass harder and sucks at my collarbone.

"Best argument ever," he murmurs.

The elevator dings and the doors slide open. "We should totally argue some more when we get back."

Grabbing my hand, we head to the car. "Deal."

Cavenite Entertainment is housed in one of the tallest buildings in down town Indianapolis. Wyatt parks in an underground parking garage and leads me inside. The two security guards working the desk pause from checking the plastic, laminated ID's of the people entering long enough to nod and smile at us.

When we reach the elevators, they pop open and we stand aside for a group of employees to rush past. Despite Wyatt's reassurance, I still feel like I stick out worse than a dick in a convent. The women are dressed in designer business attire and all of them wear heels while the men wear expensive suits similar to the one Wyatt wore when I met him. It's like you can smell the money the second you step near them.

I suppose I shouldn't worry. After the first few days in Morganville, Wyatt ditched the suit for more casual clothes like the ones he's wearing now and he seems completely comfortable. Of course, he's the owner's son, he could probably walk in wearing swim trunks and clown makeup and they'd still nod respectfully.

A tall blonde with the figure of a supermodel steps out last and her face lights up with a smile. "Wyatt! I was wondering about you. I'm glad to see you're back." She sticks her lips out in a pout I'm assuming she thinks is sexy. "We should get together again this weekend."

Her eyes scan over me as she speaks, and she sneers, taking in my plain brown hair and casual clothes. Standing up straight, I look her in the eye. I might feel a little self-conscious and out of my element here, but I know her type. No stuck-up bitch is going to make me feel small.

Wyatt must understand what she's doing as well because he drapes his arm around my waist when he replies. "It's nice to see you again, Ms. Fredericks, but as you can see, my social calendar is full at the moment. If you'll excuse us."

Without giving her a chance to respond, we step into the elevator. A smile creeps across my face at the sight of the outraged expression on hers, and I can't resist a little wave as the doors close.

"An old friend of yours?" I tease, poking him in the side.

"An old mistake. I took her out two years ago and she's never let me forget it. Vapid bitch." His palm travels across his forehead.

"Wyatt!"

"Seriously, she asked me what the name of the ship was in the Titanic movie."

We're still laughing when the doors open into a massive lobby. Another blonde sits at the expansive desk and she smiles like she's hit a lottery when she sees Wyatt. Yeah, this is pretty much what I expected.

"Ms. Lincoln, how are you?" he greets.

"I'm just fine. It's good to see you again. Your father didn't mention you were coming."

"That's all right, Kelly," a gruff voice interrupts. My head spins to see a bulky man, maybe sixty years old, with salt and pepper hair. Smiling at us, he gestures for us to follow him. "Come on in. We have a few minutes before the board meeting."

So, this is his father. I can see the resemblance. They have the same copper colored eyes that can't decide whether they're brown or gold. After we're lead into a large, plush office, Wyatt introduces us.

"Cassidy, I'd like you to meet my father, Adam Cavenite. Dad, this is Cassidy West."

"It's nice to meet you Mr. Cavenite," I say, shaking his outstretched hand.

"Please, call me Adam. I hear you're Wyatt's right hand woman at his new store."

"I'm very happy to have the opportunity."

Wyatt gestures for me to sit and then takes a seat in the chair beside me. Adam sits back with a little smirk on his face.

"So, burned down after a month, huh? You ready to try a different area? A little more populated?" The self-satisfaction in his voice makes me cringe. He actually sounds happy that his son's venture is struggling.

Wyatt seems unperturbed. "Not at all. I'm waiting to hear from the building inspector and I'll get busy rebuilding. We'll be open again in six weeks or so, I'd estimate."

Adam shakes his head. "Stubborn until the end."

"We're nowhere near the end. My Faristown location is doing well, turning a profit, and based on the first month's sales in Morganville, the new store will be even more successful."

"If you can keep it standing."

"A minor setback," Wyatt insists.

The tension in the room is suffocating as they fall quiet and proceed to stare one another down. The voice of the Animal Channel narrator plays in my head.

Here you see the alpha male in its natural habitat, facing down an offspring to show he's still dominant, but the aggression is wasted on the next generation, as he's poised to replace the aging pack leader.

Finally, Wyatt gets to his feet and holds out his hand to me. "Cass, I'll show you to our lounge where you can wait for me. I have to attend a board meeting."

"It was nice meeting you, Ms. West," Adam says, stressing my name to draw attention to the fact that Wyatt called me Cass.

"You too," I mumble as we leave.

"Sorry about that," Wyatt says as soon as we're out of earshot. "My father is a little...intense."

"It's fine."

I'm guided to the empty lounge which boasts a comfortable couch, a shiny wooden table and chairs, kitchenette, and a giant television. "There are plenty of drinks and snacks in the fridge," he tells me while handing me the TV remote. "I'll be back in less than an hour. I promise."

His shoulders are hunched a bit and his face is drawn. I've never seen him so tense, even when Scarlet Toys was burning. Before he can rush off, I slide my arms around his waist and hug him. "Don't worry about me. I'm fine right here. Go do what you need to do. Show them you've got this. Then I'll reward you when we get back to your place."

His arms tighten around me for a few seconds before he looks down at me. His face relaxes into a smile and he kisses my forehead. "You're too damn good for me. An hour and we're out of here, sweetheart."

The endearment is still ringing in my ears when he leaves.

I have the lounge to myself for the entire hour until Wyatt returns. I spend most of the time on my phone, looking for some new patterns and ideas for stuffed animals. There's a really cute snow leopard design, but I might have trouble finding the material.

My mom loved to sew and after she made me a little stuffed kitten when I was nine, I begged her to teach me. I've been making animals ever since.

Wyatt appears in the doorway, his posture tense. "Ready to go?" he asks, forcing a smile.

I wonder why he wants to be in charge here when the whole place seems to stress him out. "Sure. Are you okay?"

"I'm good. I'm ready to get you home and in my bed."

"We might need to eat at some point."

Wyatt shoots me a devious grin as we step out of the elevator into the parking garage. "That's the plan."

"Food," I laugh. "I'm going to need some actual sustenance to keep up with you."

His car glides smoothly onto the highway. "I know a good Italian place that has take-out."

"Sounds good to me."

For some reason, I expected a high scale restaurant, but he pulls into a little hole-in-the-wall place near his apartment. It smells amazing inside and the woman who waits on us is pleasant and friendly.

"Your usual?" she asks Wyatt.

He looks down at me. "I usually get a half and half. Half spaghetti and half alfredo. They also have delicious ravioli and tetrazzini if you'd rather try that."

"I'll just have what you're having. I'm not picky."

"Double my usual, plus garlic bread," he tells her, and she jots it down before heading in the back.

There are a couple of ancient arcade video games tucked into the corner and I grin when I see a tabletop version of Tetris where two players can compete. My mom had an old gaming system and I played Tetris until my hands were numb.

"Want to play?" I ask, digging a few quarters from my pocket.

His lip turns up in a smirk. "Tetris?"

"Hey, if you aren't any good at it..." I shrug and walk toward the machine.

He drops into the chair across from me. "Play until they call our name? Highest score wins?"

"You're on."

We plunk in the quarters and hit start at the same time. Now, I know Wyatt is a gamer, judging by the multiple systems in his living room, but Tetris is a little before his time and way before mine. I'm counting on that little fact to give me an advantage.

And it does.

While he watches carefully to line up each piece, I instantly turn and drop mine, leaving an open space on the end while I set up for a Tetris. Wyatt peeks over at my screen and scoffs. I'm sure it looks like I'm losing since I've built up over half of the screen. His smug look fades when I finally get the lines I've been waiting for.

Three in a row. Bam Bam Bam. Three Tetris's.

The machine plays the little tone and moves onto the next level. By the time the woman calls his name, I'm three levels ahead of him and not even breaking a sweat. It's been a while since I played, but it's still second nature to me.

"Keep going," he encourages, standing behind me with our food.

"Nah, we'll be here all night. My personal best was level twenty." I stand up and push my chair in, letting the pieces build up until the game ends.

"So, do you like any games from this decade?" he asks as we get back on the road.

"My mom had an old game system. It's the only one I've ever tried to play. I've never really been into it, but I'd give it a try." I grin at him. "You just want to play a game where I won't wipe the floor with you."

"Guilty." His lips twitch. "I'd also like to see what you could do on a first-person shooter. You have fast reflexes."

When we get inside his apartment, he places the bag of food on the counter, and I make a quick detour to use his bathroom. As I'm stepping back through the door, an arm wraps around me from behind, and his warm breath is in my ear.

"The food can wait," he murmurs. "You're too sexy. I can't stand it."

"Wow, Tetris really turns you on," I giggle, tilting my head to give him better access to my neck.

"You really turn me on."

After a thoroughly satisfying hour in Wyatt's huge bed, and another quickie in his shower that could double as a roman bath, my stomach gives a loud growl.

"Hands off, you sex fiend. I'm starving," I tell him when he runs his palm between my legs.

Wyatt's hand grabs mine as I'm stepping out of the shower. "Are you going to leave me in here all alone?"

"I'm sure you'll survive while I heat up our food."

"Ditched for a plate of spaghetti," he teases, stepping back into the spray and grabbing a bottle of shampoo.

It isn't until I'm in his kitchen that I remember it's like the command center of a damned space ship. I have no idea how to work any of this shit. Thankfully, they apparently can't make a microwave too fancy for me to figure out so I manage to heat up our pasta, but the toaster oven is another story.

It's one of those toaster/ convection / infrared / rotisserie / so smart it could probably overthrow the human race type of contraptions. I'm at a loss looking at all the dials and temperature controls.

Wyatt struts in the room wearing a pair of sweat pants, his hair still damp. "I was going to heat up the bread, but I have no idea how to work this," I confess.

"It's voice activated. Just tell it what to do."

Seriously? The lives of rich people are so different.

Wyatt walks into the pantry while I put two pieces of bread into the little metal beast. After closing the door, I say, "Toast."

Nothing happens. It's not even warming up.

"Turn on. Heat."

Again nothing.

"On, damn it!"

Is there a certain word to make it work? "Dick," I grumble. I turn around to call for Wyatt and find him standing in the doorway, his entire body shaking with laughter.

Fuck. I'm an idiot.

"You asshole!" I exclaim, shoving him.

His words come out in little gasps. "I couldn't help myself. I didn't think you'd really do it."

"Look at this place! Voice activation wasn't hard to believe."

He runs a hand through his hair, still laughing at me. "You called my toaster a dick."

"I hate you." I'm sure he doesn't believe that since I can't suppress my smile.

His arms wrap around my middle, pulling my back to his chest and he kisses the top of my head. "No, you don't."

"I'll get you back. You'll never see it coming."

"I look forward to it."

He walks over and turns a few knobs on the oven, and it starts to glow. "Plates are in that cabinet," he says, gesturing.

"Let me guess, I need a password, or maybe I have to touch it three times or some bullshit?" I giggle.

"Nah, you just have to be naked."

Shooting him a dirty look, I grab two plates from the cabinet. He places two sets of silverware beside them and pours us both a drink. It's silent for a few minutes while we both dig into the food.

"So, is everything okay at work?"

"Everything's fine. Same as usual."

"Your dad really wants to win, doesn't he?" I know they have a little bet, but I figured it was just a father's way of challenging his son, letting him test his skills before he takes charge, but after today's meeting, I don't think so. It seemed like he genuinely wanted Wyatt to fail.

"Picked up on that, huh?" Wyatt takes a bite, then sits back. "He'd rather my brother, Vince, take over when he retires, but Vince isn't interested in any of it. He's an artist with no desire to run a business. So, he's stuck with me. He's not crazy about my ideas though, so if this venture fails, he assumes I'll give up and do things his way." He grins at me. "Not going to happen. If I'm running the business, then I'm running it my way."

I understand what he's saying, but it's still sad. "Does it bother you that he's rooting for you to fail?"

"No, it just makes me try harder." My glass clinks as he refills it. "You've never told me about your family. I know you said your mother passed, but do you see your dad? Have any brothers or sisters?"

"I don't know my father. He bailed when I was a toddler. Mom was an only child and so am I, so I don't have any relatives."

Wyatt blinks and gazes at me. "That has to be tough. Having no family."

"I don't really think about it. I have good friends, and I assume I'll have a family of my own when I'm ready." Wiping my mouth with my napkin, I turn the subject back to him. "What about your mother? Is she in the picture?"

"She lives in California. They divorced a few years ago and she moved in with a guy. I see her a few times a year, holidays and such."

He gets to his feet and puts our plates into the dishwasher. Turning to me with a grin, he asks, "Do you want to tell it to wash?"

I throw a dishtowel at him. "Just keep it up. Payback is almost as big a bitch as me."

We spend the rest of the evening watching movies on his ridiculously huge television before heading to bed in the early hours of the morning. He's a natural night owl, just like me.

We sleep until nearly noon, and pack up to head to his cabin on Monroe Lake. Wyatt is in a good mood, maybe because he heard back from the building inspector and insurance company. It looks like we'll be back in business in about a month.

When we pull into the long, wooded drive that leads to his cabin, his shoulders soften and he seems as relaxed as I've ever seen him. All that ambition must be stressful.

The cabin is modest sized and all the furniture has obviously been chosen with comfort in mind. "I love it," I exclaim, falling back onto the king-sized bed.

"You haven't seen the view yet."

I follow him out to the back deck and I instantly know I'm never going to want to leave this place. Clear water reflects the blue of the sky, with tiny sparkles caught from the sun. His deck steps lead down to the bank where a kayak bobs beside a small dock. The lake is surrounded by woods, broken only by a few other houses.

"It's beautiful," I breathe.

He takes a deep breath. "I love it here, especially in the late summer when the city is sweltering."

I take a seat at the patio table while he messes with a grill in the corner. "How do you like your steak?"

"Medium. Is there anything I can do to help?"

"You can grab a few potatoes from the bin in the kitchen."

While I'm wrapping the potatoes in foil, he throws the steaks on the grill. "Do you like fish?"

"Sure."

He turns and grins at me. "If we can catch a few tonight, I'll grill them tomorrow."

"I've never been fishing before. Sounds fun."

Dinner is delicious. I swear I'm going to keep him around just to cook me steak. I'm a little surprised when he pulls out a joint as the sun goes down. I know he said he smokes occasionally, but I've never seen him. I guess this is the perfect place for it though.

We sit and watch the sun go down while we smoke.

"Still want to learn to fish?" he asks.

I assumed he meant during the day, but why not?

"Yeah, let's do it."

What was I thinking?

I'm so far outside of my comfort zone here, it's barely a speck in the distance. I'm a city girl. I grew up in a big city, then moved to the small town. At no point have I been out in the woods or at a lake at night.

You know that beautiful, glittery water I described when I first saw it? It's somehow become a flat black expanse with god only knows what horrors lurking beneath the surface. Maybe it's the little bit of weed we smoked or just the fact that I'm a foot away from the edge of the dock and one trip could see me plunged into the dark abyss that surrounds me, but it's seriously creepy.

Wyatt hands me a fishing pole with the hook already

baited. "What are you grinning about?" he asks, smiling.

"Just resisting the urge to make a master baiter joke. You'll have to show me what to do. I have no idea what I'm doing."

His chest is warm against my back as he steps up and puts a hand over mine, guiding me and demonstrating how to cast. "Now, watch the bobber," he says, pointing to the tiny orange dot. "If it dips under, jerk the line, then reel it in."

Okay, sounds simple enough.

Wyatt bends over and digs through the tackle box looking for something, and I take the opportunity to admire his ass in the moonlight. It's eerily quiet for a minute until Wyatt calls out, startling me. "You have a bite! Reel it in!"

Damn it. I was supposed to be watching the bobber, not his ass. I quickly start reeling and I can feel the resistance against the line, although it isn't strong. A few seconds before my catch breaks the water, I sort of...panic.

I blame the weed for the sudden fear that I'm going to pull some freaky huge creature bred in nuclear waste from the dark depths. I shove the pole into Wyatt's stomach. "You do it!"

Deep laughter echoes across the lake as he takes it and turns the reel a few more times. My laughter mixes with his when the killer mutant creature breaks the surface of the water. It bears a suspicious resemblance to a tiny fish.

He unhooks it and holds up the pitiful little thing. "Want a picture with this monster?"

"Shut up."

He thrusts the fish towards me, opening and closing its mouth with his finger. "Aw, don't be mean. I didn't mean to scare you. Give me a kiss."

Giggling, I grab the fish from his hand and toss it back into the water. "I'm not scared of a fish."

"So you just threw the pole at me for shits and giggles?" he teases.

"Hey, it's dark as a damn pocket out here. You can't get a city girl high and then surround her with dark water. I was waiting for a sea monster to surface."

His chest vibrates as he wraps his arms around me. "Nah,

they only live in salt water. Here you only have to worry about piranhas or gators."

"There are no gators in southern Indiana!"

"Fine, but there are catfish big enough to bite off an appendage or two."

"Very funny," I grumble, taking my pole back. "Give me a worm. I want to try again."

The worm freaks out when I pierce it with the hook and I almost drop it, but I'm determined not to freak out over something stupid again. Wyatt watches as I bait the hook and nods after I cast the line again. "Good job. Just try not to cross the lines."

"Or all life as we know it will stop instantaneously, and every molecule in your body will explode at the speed of light?"

His lips raise in a crooked grin. "Just watch your bobber, Egon."

I love how he doesn't seem affected by my weirdness. I just threw a fishing pole at him, then quoted Ghostbusters and he seems genuinely amused. It's rare to find someone who really gets you, but I think he does.

Wyatt gets his own line in the water, and we sit side by side on the dock. I finally start to relax and soak in our surroundings. Bright stars hang overhead, so vibrant and gorgeous, I just want to reach out and grab one. A slight breeze kicks up, making the water lap against the bank in a soothing rhythm.

My attention returns to the water just in time for me to see the bobber dip below the surface. "I got one. What do I do?" I exclaim, jumping to my feet.

"Yank the line to get it hooked, then reel it in." Wyatt stands beside me and breaks into laughter again when I pull the line out of the water to reveal another tiny fish.

"Hey, it's not like you're catching anything!" I giggle. This is actually fun. I've never really understood why people would like fishing, but I get it now. It's relaxing and peaceful, but exciting when you catch one.

He shows me how to get the fish off the hook, then tosses it back.

I bait the hook and cast again and I swear the line barely touches the water when I have another bite.

And another, even smaller fish.

"It's not funny," I insist, fighting back a giggle. It is, though. It is funny. Especially when it happens again.

And again.

By now, Wyatt isn't even trying not to laugh.

"I give up," I tell him, tossing the pole aside.

"Probably a good decision. We might want to leave a few baby fish in the lake."

"I'll just gather up all these huge catfish that you caught...wait a minute..." I look around like I've lost something. "Where did they all go?"

"Probably busy taking care of all the injured children."

"Don't say that!" I exclaim, shoving him.

I swear I didn't mean to push him hard. I don't know if I'm unaware of my own strength or his balance sucks, but he trips, drops the pole and stumbles off the dock and into the water.

Oh god. I killed him.

I pushed him into the black water and he's going to be eaten by the Lochness monster. The water bubbles where he went under.

"Wyatt!" I scream. Oh shit. He's not coming back up. What if he can't swim? I'm not a strong swimmer and I have no idea how deep the water is.

The longest thirty seconds of my life passes as I repeatedly call his name. Finally, I hear a chuckle coming from behind me and spin around so fast, my vision takes a second to focus on the dark figure standing shoulder deep in the water beside the opposite side of the dock.

Okay, so the water isn't deep.

"That wasn't funny!"

"Hey, you shoved me in." He climbs out, raining drops onto the wooden dock.

"It was an accident! I thought you drowned or something!"

He reaches out and grabs me, pulling me against his soaked body. "Aw, were you worried about me?" he teases.

"You'd better be worried about your balls if you pull any shit like that again." I can't help the smile on my face. "Now let me go. You smell like old fish."

His smile widens, and we head back up toward the cabin. "You're awfully judgmental for a baby fish murderer."

The next few days are a glorious mixture of relaxation, sex, swimming, sex, laughing, and sex. It's the best vacation I've ever had and I could spend the rest of my life hiding away in this cabin with Wyatt. Too bad we'll have to get back to life eventually.

I'm standing in the kitchen, trying to decide what to make for dinner while Wyatt paces back and forth across the back deck.

Whoever he's talking to on the phone isn't telling him anything he wants to hear. His hand runs through his hair and he blows air through his lips before ending the call.

"Is everything okay? Is the rebuilding not going well on the store?" I ask when he steps inside.

"Our store is fine, but it looks like I have an issue at the one in Tennessee. The books show everything is fine, but sales took a deep dip for no apparent reason. It looks like someone has been stealing." He cocks his eyebrow at me. "Are you up for another road trip?"

"Sure, but if you'd rather handle it on your own, you can drop me home on the way."

He steps up behind me and plants a kiss on the back of my neck. "I want you to come with me."

God, he can drive me crazy with the smallest touch. "Fine, but you know the rules. If you kiss my neck, you have to put out."

The words are barely out of my mouth when I'm bent over the counter, my panties at my feet and my shirt shoved up my back. I hear the crinkle of the condom wrapper before his fingers dip inside me. "You always have a condom within reach," I giggle.

"I'm travelling with a beautiful woman who has an ass I want to bite." His palm leaves a sting on my cheek. "I'm not missing out on an opportunity."

Light kisses down my spine halt my giggles, and I groan as he sinks in so damn deep. My feet dangle an inch above the kitchen tile, and I hold onto the far edge of the counter like it's trying to escape as he pounds into me.

His hands grip my hips and he lifts me a bit, adjusting his angle and hitting a spot that makes me cry out.

"Right there, huh," he murmurs.

"Yes! Fuck! Don't…"

My words are stolen by the powerful spasms seizing my body, and all I can do is ride it out, reveling in the heat streaking across my skin. I swear this man is a fucking voodoo sex sorcerer. No one else can draw these reactions from my body, not even me.

Soft kisses fall on my neck and shoulders and I hum. My voice shakes a little when I say, "Well, that was unexpected."

"You asked for it, baby. I'm always a second away from fucking you. Anytime and anywhere you want it."

And there goes my vagina, planning a future with him when my brain knows it's all temporary.

After a quick shower, we get packed and head out for the drive down to Tennessee.

Scarlet Toys South, as Wyatt has been calling it, is a little larger than the one I manage. It makes sense I guess, since the city is a bit more populated as well.

"I'm not sure they count as a small town if their McDonalds is open twenty-four hours," I point out as we park just outside the back entrance.

"The one in Morganville closes?"

"At ten. We do have a supercenter though."

"Moving up in the world," he chuckles, grabbing my hand as we head inside.

I'm a little surprised. I assumed he'd want to remain professional here, at his other place of business. Maybe he just isn't going to mention I manage the other Scarlet Toys.

A bell goes off as we step inside and a petite, dark headed woman glances up at us. She does a quick double take, then quickly straightens her spine and rushes around the counter.

"Wyatt, I didn't know you were coming."

"Surprise." He walks over to the counter and gestures to me. "Cass, this is Joanne Michaels, assistant manager of Scarlet Toys South. Joanne, this is Cassidy West, General manager of Scarlet Toys North."

The smile on her face is as fake as her eyelashes when she replies, "It's so nice to meet you." A slight frown creases her lips as she notices he hasn't released my hand. "And I told you to call me JoJo."

Wyatt only grins in response before asking, "Is Diana off tonight?"

"She left a few minutes ago. Do you want me to call her?"

"That's not necessary. I know where she keeps the books. We'll be in the office."

Joanne twists the ring on her finger and her voice wobbles a little as she asks, "Is everything okay?"

The smile on Wyatt's face isn't one I've seen before. It's forced, and I realize what I'm seeing is anger, bubbling just under the surface. "Everything's fine. Just checking in, routine stuff."

Joanne's head bobs and her shoulders relax a little. A customer approaches the counter, so her attention is diverted as we head back to the office.

"You think she's the one?" I whisper, taking a seat in an office twice the size of the one at my store.

"I do now. She doesn't exactly have a poker face, does she?"

"She went from eye fucking you to fidgeting pretty fast."

A thought jumps into my head as Wyatt pulls out a stack of paperwork. "Did you fuck her too? She's a manager. Are you a serial manager fucker, Wyatt?"

A snorting laugh escapes him. "No, I don't have a manager fetish." His lips cock up in a little smirk. "Are you jealous, Cassidy?"

Damn it.

"Of course not."

"Uh-huh." I want to smack that satisfied little grin off his face.

I lean my chair back and gaze around the room. "Don't

worry. I know this is just temporary. I'm not reading more into it."

My breath catches when he grabs the arms of the chair and leans on them, bringing the feet back to the ground and damn near giving me a heart attack. "Asshole! I thought I was going to fall."

His eyes are intense as they focus on mine. "Who said this is temporary?"

"You're only in town for a few months. And I said I wasn't looking for anything serious."

"Doesn't matter what you're looking for. That's not how it works. When something good falls into my path, I don't veer around it."

Is he saying what I think he is? "And I'm...something good?" I murmur.

I'm still pinned in by his arms, his eyes burning into mine. "You're something amazing. Funny and smart, hardworking and beautiful. And you actually care about other people. That's a rare combination, so don't tell me that this is temporary. Tell me this is something you want as much as I do."

I'm caught up in his words and the intensity of his gaze as he waits for me to answer. "You want a real relationship," I finally state.

"We have a real relationship. I want you to know our real relationship doesn't have an expiration date."

"Okay."

Standing up, he grins at me. "Okay? That's all I get?"

"What? You need to hear me say that I think you're sweet, you make me laugh, and I love every minute I spend with you even when we're just lying around doing nothing?" I tease, getting to my feet and looping my arms around his neck.

His hands land on my hips and he pulls me against him. "And I'm devastatingly hot, don't forget that."

"Yeah, I guess you're kind of cute."

"Cute! Bunnies are cute. Puppies are cute. I'm—"

"Hey, don't get ahead of yourself. I didn't say you were as cute as a bunny. That's a pretty high bar. A puppy, maybe. Unless it's one who trips over his ears then—"

His lips land on mine, soft but demanding, and I groan as he slips his tongue against mine and kisses me until every inch of my skin feels alive and tingly. Somehow, I end up with a handful of his ass because I swear my hands have a mind of their own.

"You want to try that again?" he breathes in my ear after we break apart.

"Fine, you're sexy as fuck and every time you walk into a room I want to take my panties off."

"That's more like it." He swats me on the ass.

"So, we're officially together?" I clarify.

"Yes." He gathers up some receipts and papers. "Now let's go to the hotel so you can get some rest while I catch a thief."

Joanne eyes us warily when we leave. If she is the one stealing, the sight of Wyatt carrying the books and inventory sheets must scare the shit out of her.

"What's her story?" I ask as he drives us to a nearby hotel. "Do you know anything about her? Maybe she's desperate for money for some reason? Not that it would justify stealing. I just wondered." I know what it's like to struggle. What if she's stealing money to feed her kid or something?

"She's married to the chief of police and they're pretty well off. She wanted the job because her kids are grown and out of the house."

"So, she's a bored housewife?"

"Basically."

"And she probably thinks she can do whatever she wants because she's married to the chief."

Wyatt parks the car and we head inside to the rental office. "Not in my store, she can't. I do my best to support my staff, pay a fair wage with benefits, and offer flexible schedules. In return, I expect hard work and honesty. I have no sympathy for a thief. Whoever it is, I will file charges."

"You should," I agree.

Our room is a suite that takes up the top half of the third floor. I'm instantly in love with it when I find it has a huge tub with jets.

Wyatt chuckles at my enthusiasm. "Go on and have a soak.

I'm going to go through these reports and see what I can find."

He doesn't have to make that suggestion twice. Wyatt settles at a desk in the next room with his laptop and the stack of papers from the store while I fill the tub. There are tiny bottles of bath salts on the counter in the bathroom. This place is getting a fantastic review from me.

I choose a citrus scented bottle and add it to the tub before stripping down and easing into the hot water. A floor length mirror hangs on the inside of the door, so with the door open, I can see Wyatt in the reflection. His lips are pressed together as he sorts through paperwork, occasionally making notes and typing on his computer.

He has made himself comfortable, removing his shoes and socks, and changing into a t-shirt and sweats. I swear I could stare at this man until we both wither from old age. His words from earlier ring in my head and I lie back, letting myself think about how things have changed.

This isn't a fling. It isn't just a temporary fuck buddy situation and I don't really know how I feel about that. I've been worried that I was catching feelings for him, setting myself up for future heartache when he leaves, but I never considered that he might be feeling the same way. I mean, I'm no uggo, but look at him. The man could have any woman in the world. What are the chances that this is going to work?

I know I have a tendency to overthink things, to analyze them to death, and I need to stop. Some things can't be predicted. There are times when you just have to relax, wander the path and see where it spits you out. Fortunately, my path has crossed with a gorgeous, caring man with a cock that even the most uptight virgin would worship.

I'm not going to worry about what happens when he needs to go back to Indianapolis for good. Or think too much about how different our lives are and how that could possibly work. I'm just going to enjoy the ride and damn the consequences.

The hot bubbling water doesn't take long to suck away my stress and I lay my head back, closing my eyes. I don't know how much time passes before I feel like I'm being watched and drag my eyes open. I may have dozed off for a bit.

Wyatt stands in the doorway, leaning against the jamb. "You were smiling in your sleep."

"Hmm, must've been dreaming about you," I reply, stretching. "Or food. I'm starving."

Chuckling, he grabs a large, fluffy towel and walks over to me. "I just ordered a pizza. If you can tear yourself away from the bubbles."

My skin is puckered and wrinkly when I stand. "Damn, I have been in here too long. My skin looks like your balls."

"You should be honored then. My balls are very attractive." He wraps the towel around me.

"Balls are not attractive," I snort.

"Hey, you'll make them self-conscious." His hand travels down like he's comforting his nuts.

Slipping my hand down his pants, I give them a little squeeze. "Sorry, I'll be kinder to Bert and Ernie."

His fingers close over my nipple. "You are not naming my balls after Muppets."

A knock at the door interrupts us. "Guess I'll have to wait for later to play with Thing One and Thing Two. Pizza's here."

He delivers a stinging slap to my bare, wet ass. "Get dressed, baby."

Wyatt inhales two pieces of pizza before returning to the desk.

"Anything I can help with?" I ask, after tucking our leftovers into the small fridge.

"I'm missing something. It's just like Diana, the GM, said. Look." He slides the paperwork over to me. "The cash drawers aren't coming up short. Not more than a few cents here or there, which is normal. But it looks like sales have taken a sharp drop all at once. Yet, when compared to the inventory, it doesn't add up. We're selling the same amount of items for the same price, but somehow bringing in less money. I'd assume we're missing the stock from shoplifters, but not at this rate, and some of the items are too large and obvious to walk out with." He sits back and runs a hand through his hair.

I scan over the reports and inventory numbers before glancing at the pile of receipts on the edge of the desk. "What are those?"

"Voids," he says, waving his hand at them in dismissal. "I checked them against the drawer counts and it adds up."

It suddenly becomes crystal clear what's going on.

"It's a void scam."

Wyatt stares up at me. "A what?"

"Look." I gather up the receipts that have *void* written across them. "I knew someone who got fired from a fast food joint for this. When the cashier rings up a purchase, say for a hundred dollars, they keep the receipt instead of giving it to the customer. Customers almost never take a receipt from me or they toss it in the trash can by the door. No one is going to bring back a sex toy. The cashier marks the receipt as a void, as if the customer changed their mind about the purchase or forgot their money or whatever. Now, it looks like there's a hundred dollars extra in the drawer because they made a sale they're claiming was voided. All they have to do is pocket the hundred dollars and the drawer comes out even. The items are missing from inventory because they've been sold, but there's no record of it."

Wyatt thinks about it for a minute. "I have cameras pointed at the cash register. Diana didn't check them because the drawers weren't coming up short." He leaps to his feet and starts throwing on clothes. "I'm going to check the feeds."

"I'm coming with you."

I look through the voids on the drive over and notice something that really sucks. "I might be wrong," I mumble. "The whole void scam is usually pulled by a cashier, but these receipts are from three different employees. I can't imagine they all know how to do this."

"We'll see," he grunts.

He doesn't say another word until we get out of the car. "They better not have changed the alarm code."

Wyatt unlocks the door, enters the code into the alarm keypad, and we make our way into the darkened store. I flip on the lights while he retrieves two flash drives from the office and plugs his laptop in on the counter.

I grab two stools, and we sit down to watch the world's most boring reality show.

"Jesus, does he ever stop picking his nose?" Wyatt scoffs, grimacing.

"When customers are present," I giggle. It's amazing what people do when they think no one can see them. They obviously forgot that the camera was watching.

The grossest moment was actually from a customer. The cashier stepped out of view to fetch something and the woman took the opportunity to scratch between her legs and promptly smell her fingers.

"Oh, another scratch and sniff," I exclaim, shaking my head.

Wyatt regards me. "*Another*?"

"We had a girl on the circle that used to do that. She'd scratch her crotch or her ass and then smell her hand. Some kids called her out on it once and she told them it was to make sure her underwear was fresh. They dubbed her scratch and sniff from then on. She moved a while back."

Wyatt stares at me like he thinks I'm screwing with him, then bursts into laughter. "That neighborhood of yours, I swear."

"Life on the circle." I shrug. "It's not always pretty."

After another hour of zooming through tapes and watching the boring transactions, Wyatt rubs a palm over his face. "I don't see anything. No one has even opened the drawer without a sale. Unless someone has some real slight of hand, we're missing something."

The corner of one of the voided receipts catches my eye and it all makes sense. "It's not the cashiers," I exclaim, snatching up a few more receipts. "Look."

Wyatt's brow creases as I point out a small number two in the corner of the receipt. It's easy to miss if you aren't looking for it since it blends in with the date. "What am I looking at?"

"That little two means this was the second receipt printed for that sale."

"You can print two receipts?"

"Yes, let's say the paper ran out or jammed and the receipt didn't print. Or the customer lost it and wants another copy. All you have to do is go into the system and reprint it. The only difference will be the small two, that shows it's a copy and not the original. Plus, the time stamp shows when the copy was printed, not the original."

Wyatt leans an elbow on the counter. "Then they voided the second receipt and took the money. Do all the cashiers know how to do this?"

"No!" I'm so excited I hop off of the stool. "That's the point. None of them can. Only someone with the manager code can reprint the receipts. Who has the code?"

Wyatt's lips press together. "Joanne and Diana. Diana is the one who reported the discrepancies."

"So, it's Joanne, like you suspected. All she had to do was wait until everyone went home at night. Reprint receipts from multiple transactions throughout the day, then void them, and take the money from the cash drawers. The drawers would never be short, the inventory would, and overall sales would fall." I sort through the receipts in his hand. "Look, they were all printed within minutes of each other, and all after hours."

Wyatt takes the last set of receipts and forwards the video to the time stamped on it. Sure enough, Joanne stands at the register, printing off copies of the receipts. She gathers them up and takes the cash drawer back to the office. When Wyatt switches to the recording from the office camera, there's no doubt left.

She adds up the receipt totals and puts the money in a separate deposit envelope from the rest of the profits. Once everything is put away and locked up, she tucks both envelopes in her purse. "One for the bank and one for her," I murmur.

Wyatt grabs me and plants a kiss on my lips. "You're a genius."

"Nah, above average, at most." I flop my hand at him. "It's the multitude of voided receipts that gave it away. I get two voids a week at most, not five or more per day. She's really been cutting into your profit."

"Not anymore," he growls. "I'm filing a police report first thing in the morning." He grabs Joanne's personnel file and dials her number from the store phone.

"Wyatt, it's three a.m."

"See how many shits I give," he mumbles. "Joanne? Yes, it's Wyatt and I'm sure you know why I'm calling. I want your keys to the store in the drop box within the next hour or there will be officers sent to your house. You are barred from the property, and I wouldn't expect a final check since it appears you've taken far more than any wages I'd owe you. One hour." He hangs the phone up without giving her a chance to reply.

I've never heard him talk to anyone that way. So forceful and commanding. Still seething, he turns to me and his face softens, a smirk working its way through to the surface. "Cass?"

"Hmm?"

"Want to tell me why you're looking at me like that?"

Trying to pull myself together, I take a step back. "I wasn't looking at you."

"Uh-huh, and I guess you aren't rubbing your thighs together while your nipples try to pierce through your shirt either."

Traitor nipples.

"Definitely not."

His arms shoot out and I'm pulled against him, my back to his chest. His voice is hot in my ear. "You like it when I give orders? I think it gets you all worked up."

"Yes," I admit.

"Oh, babe. I'll remember that." He reaches for a small plastic paddle and dangles it in front of my face. "I'd love to give orders to a naughty employee."

Holy shit. What did I just start? "Well, if we're going to incorporate toys, I may have a few ideas as well."

Chuckling, he kisses my ear then hands me a bag. "Fill it up. I'm open minded."

A smile crawls across my face. "Anything I want to try, huh?"

"Anything. I'm going to get these papers together and turn

the cameras back on. Then we'll go."

A loud clunk sounds from just outside, followed by the sound of an engine revving. "That was fast," I remark.

"She probably assumes I won't press charges if she does what I tell her."

"But you're going to?"

"You can bet your sweet little ass on it. Go get your toys and let's get out of here. I'm exhausted."

A yawn escapes me. "Me too." Wyatt isn't paying any attention to what I grab so I can't resist throwing in a little something to tease him with.

We crash as soon as we get back to the hotel and sleep late. When I wake, Wyatt is sitting on the edge of the bed with a devious grin on his face. The bag from Scarlet Toys is in his hands.

"I have to say, Cass, I'm a little surprised. Who knew you were so kinky?"

"I'm not kinky! I've never used any of that stuff before." His eyes zero in on my bare breasts when the blanket falls away as I sit up. He pulls out a pair of pink, fluffy handcuffs.

"You'd let me cuff you?"

"Would you want to?"

"Fuck yeah."

"I mainly got them to cuff you, actually."

His eyebrows shoot up. "Oh really?"

"Yep." I crawl down the bed and dig into the bag. "It'll keep you from squirming too much when I use this." I pull out a slim, strap-on dildo and swing it in front of his face.

I swear I can practically hear his asshole pucker shut. "No way. Noooo. Not happening."

"What happened to being open minded?"

"My mind is open. My ass is closed. Padlocked shut with a giant *exit only* sign."

"Hmm, too bad. And I was going to let you try out that paddle."

"I'm bigger than you, babe. I can paddle your plump little ass whenever the mood strikes me."

Yeah, that threat shouldn't turn me on the way it does.

Shit, I guess I am kinky. My reaction doesn't escape his notice, and his grin broadens. Before he can say anything, there's a curt knock at our door.

A young man calls out, "Housekeeping!" as he enters. It takes a second for him to notice we're still in the room. Probably because it's past checkout time and we shouldn't be.

His gaze lands first on the bed that is covered in an array of sex toys. Then his stunned eyes turn to me, and I squeal with the sudden realization I'm bare assed and holding a dildo in my hand.

"I'll c-come back," he stammers and flees the room.

Wyatt bursts out laughing, shaking the bed as I jump up and get dressed, my face burning red. "It's not funny! He probably thinks I'm a hooker!" I cry, which just makes him laugh harder.

"Fine," I reply, trying not to smile. "No paddle for you."

I barely have the words out when I find myself flung across his knee. "Oh really? So, what's this in my hand then?" He flips my skirt up, exposing my panties.

Why did I choose a skirt?

"You better never!"

Cold, smooth plastic rubs circles on my ass cheeks as I struggle to get up. "Now, fighting isn't going to help. You let another man see your ass when it belongs to me. I'd say that's worth at least five swats, but since it's your first time, I'll knock it down to three."

"Wyatt, I swear to fuck if you—"

Swat!

It startles me more than it stings, and I feel my face ignite again. It's the strangest sensation, being over his knee like this. Even though we're just teasing, it's a feeling of vulnerability I'm not used to.

"I'm going to kill you!"

Swat! Ow, okay, that one stung.

"Did that hurt?" he taunts, rubbing my ass.

"No! But when I get up—"

"It didn't hurt? Okay, then." His fingers slide under my panties, slipping them down my legs. I swear my face is going to combust.

S.M. SHADE

But apparently not as quickly as my ass because that little plastic paddle burns like hell when it slaps against my bare ass. "Wyatt!" I squeal, and he pulls my panties back up.

He lets me up and as much as I want to glare at him, I can't look at him. I'm too embarrassed. When I turn my back and reach for my shoes, he wraps his arms around me from behind.

"You have the sexiest, most spankable ass I've ever seen," he murmurs in my ear. Apparently, embarrassment doesn't outweigh the effect he always has on me, and I can feel my insides clench at the sound of his voice.

"I can't believe you did that!" I exclaim, stepping out of his embrace.

"Are you upset because I spanked you or because you liked it?" I can't seem to find any words, so he spins me around and pinches my chin between his thumbs, forcing me to look at him. "Talk to me, Cass."

Shrugging, I mumble, "It's embarrassing."

His warm arms wrap around me. "You never have to be embarrassed with me. Whatever we do stays between us." He grins down at me. "Besides, you were the one threatening to penetrate my ass."

"Not threatening, promising," I correct, and he shakes his head.

He drops a quick kiss on my lips. "We'd better get out of here before that boy comes back hoping for another show."

Chapter Six

The next two weeks seem to fly by. Wyatt stays with me instead of returning to his hotel, and I'm impressed with how unfazed he seems with the normal Violent Circle hijinks. The man is nothing if not adaptable.

The Scarlet Toys building is being repaired and remodeled with amazing speed and it looks like we'll be able to start stocking the merchandise again in a week or so.

Wyatt has to go back to Tennessee to give a deposition about the theft, and even though he invites me, I decide to stay home this time.

"I haven't seen much of Jani lately. We're going to spend Saturday together, hit the mall, get our hair done, you know, girly stuff. Jani's happy we're dating, you know."

"Doesn't keep her from flirting with me," he points out.

"Actually, now she's just talking about a threesome."

Wyatt's head whips around, and I hold up my palm. "Don't even think about it."

"You wouldn't want to try it?"

"A threesome? Hmm...depends on which one of your friends."

"My friends!"

"Or I still have your little friend under my mattress," I tease. The strap on dildo has been there since we returned.

Chuckling, he leans down and kisses me. "All I need is you, babe. I'll see you the day after tomorrow."

"Be careful," I call as I follow him outside.

Jani is just coming up the walk. "Don't worry! I'll take her to the spa. Get her jungle deforested before you get back!" she shouts as if the whole damn neighborhood can't hear.

Wyatt just gives her a wave and takes off. He might be getting too used to our insanity.

"Well, come on hussy! I told Emily we'd pick her up," Jani says.

"Keep your panties on, I'm coming."

"It's not often my brother actually visits and can sit with Mom. I've gotta take my freedom while I have it."

I hop in Jani's car and we pick up Emily on the way to the strip mall. Our girl's day out might not be as fancy as some other women have, considering we're starting at a thrift store, but we have a lot of fun together. Besides, thrift stores can be a treasure trove of new brand name clothes for ridiculously low prices. It's amazing how much gets donated that still bears the original tags.

"So, have you heard from Noble since the block party?" Emily asks Jani as we head inside.

"Nope. I think he finally got the message."

"Not likely," I giggle.

"So, I hear you and Wyatt are together now?" Emily says.

"Yep," Jani interjects. "He fucked his way into her little black heart that is so determined not to love."

I shove Jani. "You're one to talk. I don't exactly see you settling down."

"When I find the right penis, I will."

We stop at the racks of skirts and dresses. "What about you, Em? Seeing anyone?"

"Do the old men who bring me their skid marked underwear to wash every week count?"

"Ugh. Gross. I don't know how you do it," Jani says.

"Two pairs of gloves. It sucks, but it pays better than retail or fast food." Emily holds up a pale blue dress. 'What do you think?"

"Makes your eyes shine," I tell her. "Get it."

"There is a guy I've had my eye on. He comes in on Sundays with about ten bags of dirty clothes and washes them himself. He's really cute, but I assume he has a family with that kind of load."

"Wedding ring?" Jani asks, returning a godawful yellow skirt to the rack.

"No, so probably a girlfriend."

"Or a boyfriend," Jani replies. "The best looking ones are usually gay. Except for Cassidy's man. Unless..." She turns and grins at me.

"Totally straight," I laugh.

"Damn, I'd be his beard any day. Sit right on his face."

Emily and I both crack up. "I don't think that's how it works."

Jani pulls out a silky, black, flared dress and practically shoves it at me. "You have to get this. It'll drive Wyatt crazy."

"You're supposed to be dressing yourself, you know."

"Yeah, but you don't have my fat ass. I'll never have your lean figure, so I'm living vicariously. Go try it on."

"Guys love your ass," I point out, before heading to the fitting room.

By the time I've changed into it, I know Jani is right. It fits perfectly and hugs my slight curves. It even fits through the chest. It's hard to find dresses that don't gape over my bitty titties, but this actually makes them look good.

We all leave the thrift store with bags of new clothes before heading to the shoe store. The key to shopping when you don't have a lot of money is to save it where you can, like shopping at a thrift store instead of a mall, so you can spend it where you want to, like the shoe store.

I'm not as shoe crazy as Jani is, but I find a new pair of sneakers to replace my worn ones and a pair of ballet flats to match my new dress. My phone beeps, and I take a seat to read my text while Jani and Emily are trying on shoes.

Wyatt: Having fun?

Me: Yeah, at the shoe store now.

Wyatt: Getting whore red stilettos?

Me: You know me so well.

Wyatt: I'm just lying in bed at the hotel. All alone. Deposition was postponed until tomorrow morning.

Me: So you're jacking off?

Wyatt: You know me so well. It would go a lot faster if you'd send me a picture.

Giggling, I snap a picture of the wall of sneakers in front of me and send it.

Wyatt: ha ha, you know what I want to see.

Me: And I'm in a shoe store.

Wyatt: That I'm sure has a restroom.

Before I can tell him to kiss my ass, Jani laughs. "Go on. I dare you. I'll bet you've never sent a nude in your life, have you?"

"Stop snooping, bitch!" I laugh, shoving her away.

"Send the poor guy a topless shot at least."

Emily joins the conversation. "Do you not trust him to keep it private?"

"He wouldn't show it to anyone." I look up at Emily. "You really think I should?"

"Why not?" She shrugs. "Tell him you want one in return."

"I already have a dick pic from him."

Jani's eyes widen. "Whip it out!"

"No!" I glance around the store. "Okay, I'm going to the restroom."

Thankfully, the restroom is empty, and I take the last of the four stalls. I whip off my shirt and take a quick picture of my chest, hitting send before I can change my mind.

The door to the restroom squeaks as it opens and I hear a woman murmur. "I swear you have to visit every bathroom in the city." She must have a kid with her.

I mute my phone just in time as Wyatt's response comes through.

Wyatt: Fuck, babe, I just want to suck those nipples.

Show me more.

I can't believe I'm sexting in a shoe store bathroom. A funny thought occurs to me. Since we're going for a wax at the day spa next, I could do a little before and after picture. Jani was right when she said I've never sent nudes before. It's time to live a little.

As quietly as possible, I put my shirt back on and slip off my panties, leaving my skirt on. Hmm...I'm not sure about the best way to do this.

I'm not going to squat down in here. I finally decide to put one foot on the toilet seat and then shove the camera under my skirt. The first picture is out of focus and with the light filtering through my green skirt, it looks more like a stepped on tennis ball than a vagina. Fine, the skirt has to come off too.

It joins my panties, hanging on the toilet paper dispenser. I've never felt so classy.

Naked from the waist down, I put my foot on the seat again, and focus on getting the perfect shot. The next one is pretty good and I send it, but I decide to take one more.

Why did I decide to take one more?

Just as I hit the button, the toilet seat slides to the side and the plastic bolts in the back holding it on both snap. The seat clatters to the floor, and my foot slides right into the toilet with a splash they probably heard on the sales floor. Thinking I'm going to fall, I panic and grab at the wall, dropping my phone, which slides out of the stall and toward the sinks.

So, there I am in all my glory. Naked, with a broken toilet seat looped around one foot while my other foot rests ankle deep in blue toilet water. No way this can get worse, right?

Wrong.

As I'm trying to extricate myself, I hear a small voice ask, "Mommy, what's that?"

"The lady dropped her phone, Justin. Just put it on the sink for her."

Oh god.

Oh no.

"But what *is* that? It's weird and...hairy."

Somebody please shoot me now. Where is a nice stroke or heart attack when you need one? Behind the door, a small boy is getting a look at his first vagina.

My vagina.

The toilet flushes and I hear his mother gasp when she takes the phone from him.

Yeah, I'm not coming out of here. Somebody is going to have to deliver my food because I'm never leaving this stall again.

"What is it?" he repeats.

"It's just, um, a close up picture," she stumbles, grasping for an explanation that isn't *some stranger's vagina.*

"Close up of what?" he insists.

"A...mouth. It's just a blurry picture." I hear the click of plastic against porcelain as she places the phone on the sink and says, "Wash your hands again."

"But I already—"

"Again, Justin!"

Justin isn't finished asking questions though. Through the running water, I hear, "It had a moustache though. And four lips! Do some guys have extra lips? Am I gonna get more lips? Ohh! Is it an alien? Aliens can have extra lips."

His voice fades as they leave, and I rush through the stall door to grab my phone, one shoe sloshing and leaving blue puddles across the floor. Of course, they had to have blue water. I pop off my shoe and stuff it with paper towels to mop up the bulk of the water.

That is how Jani and Emily find me a few seconds later.

"Uh...Cass, any idea why the manager just sent us in here to tell you to leave. Something about taking obscene pictures?" Jani asks, her lips twitching as she holds back a smile.

"Oh hell. I can't go out there!" I wail.

Emily giggles and shakes her head. "Come on. I'll walk out with you while Jani pays for our stuff. What the hell happened?"

"Oh no. Wait until I get outside too. I'm not missing this story," Jani insists.

My eyes never leave the ugly carpeted floor as I make a beeline for the door and wait in the car with Emily for Jani to show up. As we're waiting another text comes through from Wyatt.

Wyatt: So fucking hot. Put your fingers in and take a picture.

Fuming, I send a return message.

Me: Fuck off

Ever since I regaled Wyatt with the story of my catastrophic first attempt at sexting, he teases me at least once a day with a text requesting a crotch shot. Never going to happen.

Wyatt seems to have straightened out the issue at Scarlet Toys South and refocused his attention on our store. The weather has been great which has really helped with the rebuild. We've been waiting for the day when we can start restocking and prepare to open. When we finally get the call, it's accompanied by more bad news.

It's clear from Wyatt's expression that something is wrong and I sit beside him as he hangs up the phone.

"Well, we can start getting the stock moved in again," he says.

"But?"

"But the town has apparently decided to hold a vote on Proposition Four. Also known as the Children First Initiative."

Confused, I shake my head. "I've never heard of it."

He gives me a wry smile. "That's because they introduced it while we were gone. It would block any adult stores, strip clubs, or anything they consider immoral from doing business in Ashen county."

It takes a few moments for his words to sink in. Finally, I realize the repercussions of such a law and anger races through me. "Those self-righteous fuckwits!" I jump to my feet and pace the room. "Protect the children! Like we're selling dildos at the school bake sale. It doesn't have a damn thing to do with children. Maybe if they cleaned the cobwebs out of their withered up snatches, they'd lighten the fuck up!"

Wyatt's jaw falls open and he bursts out laughing.

Freezing in place, I gape at him. "This isn't funny! Your store. They're going to shut it down. It took three votes to get the county to go wet and that took five years. When those sanctimonious prudes get together, they have the numbers to stall shit for a long time."

Wyatt stands and walks over to me, still restraining his laughter. "You are so damned cute when you're pissed."

Is there anything worse than being called cute when you're angry? "It's not cute," I reply through gritted teeth.

Doesn't he understand what this means? It might not be the end of the world for him. He'll go back to his lap of luxury life in Indianapolis, or focus on his other store. I'll be out of a job I really like, but I know that isn't the main reason I'm upset.

I'll lose him.

When those stuck up bitches get their way, and run Scarlet Toys out of town, they'll be taking him away from me too.

"No, it's not cute or funny. It's going to be a pain in the ass, but that doesn't mean we can't win."

"You don't understand. They'll never quit."

His hands squeeze my shoulders and he looks me in the eye. "Neither will I."

My anger fades and fear rushes into its place as I'm struck by a realization. "I don't want to lose you. Shit...Wyatt." I pull back and pace across the room. My stomach churns and my chest feels tight. "I'm falling for you. Or I already have."

I didn't mean to tell him, but the words broke free anyway.

The next few seconds drag into months as he stares at me. I'm terrified that I've blown it. The next words out of his mouth are going to shatter me if he ends it because I just spewed feelings all over the place.

Finally, a smile blooms on his face and he walks toward me. "Cass, I'm not going anywhere, store or no store." He slides his hand behind my neck and his fingers crawl into my hair. "We're going to make this work. You aren't the only one falling." He pulls me against him, cupping the back of my head as I rest my cheek on his chest.

"I know we've only known each other a couple of months. I didn't want to scare you off by telling you. You said from the beginning you didn't want anything serious, but it doesn't change how I feel. I love you."

A sense of euphoria settles over me, and I wrap my arms around his back. "I love you, too. And it scares the hell out of me," I confess.

He steps back and sweeps the hair from my forehead as I gaze up at him. "Why?"

"I don't know. I've never been in love. I feel...deliriously happy and terrified at the same time."

Chuckling, he plants a sweet kiss on my lips. "That's a pretty good description of love."

I grin up at him. "I guess you should know since you're the old man with all the experience."

"Call me old again, and I'll have to break out the paddle."

"I haven't forgotten about that. Your day of payback is still coming," I warn. "Now, what are we going to do about Scarlet Toys?"

"I'm going to get in touch with our company's lawyers, and see what they suggest. In the meantime, we go about our business as usual." He slaps me on the ass. "So, let's go check out the building."

The smell of paint is overwhelming when we walk inside, but it's better than the smoke scent it used to have. Wyatt had them wall things off a little differently so the office is now bigger and we have a little break area on one side of the storeroom.

"We'll put a table and chairs there. Mini fridge and microwave can go in the corner. It'll make it easier on everyone to bring their lunch," he points out.

"That'll be nice," Jani pipes up, walking up behind us.

"Word travels fast, I guess," I laugh, and she shakes her head.

"I saw your car out back, Bare n' Share."

Wyatt gives her a puzzled look. "She likes to show pictures of her bare foo foo to people in women's restrooms. Gets us banned from stores."

"One store!"

She laughs as I smack her. "And it was your fault. You talked me into it!"

Jani laughs and dodges me. "Did she tell you how she got one smurf shoe?"

Wyatt cracks up. "I thought maybe she tried to flush herself to escape."

"You're going to have smurf balls if you keep it up," I warn. "Now, are we moving stuff in or what?"

"I'll get the register and everything wired in if you want to set up the display racks." He turns to Jani. "Do you want to stay and help?"

"Are you kidding? I'm going crazy being stuck at home with Mom. I'm in."

"Your mom is sweet," I tell her as we walk through the store.

"Yeah, feel free to come over and catch the four hours a day of reality television. She's driving me nuts with one that shows children's beauty pageants."

"Ugh...that's so wrong. Pitting kids against each other based on their looks. They even have them wear fake teeth! What's cuter than a little kid with missing teeth?"

"Yeah, she watches it and yells at the screen half the time about how horrible it all is." Jani follows me out to the long cargo container sitting behind the store. All the stock has been waiting here for the building to be ready.

"Then why does she watch it?"

"Exactly," she groans.

We spend the next few hours putting the store back in order. Wyatt calls Clarence and Martha to let them know they can return to work, and they promise to be in the next day. Neither of us mentions the upcoming proposition, although I know Jani is aware. For now, it's just business as usual.

It takes two weeks to get the store back up and running.

When we re-open, a giant banner hangs out front.

We're Back! Don't miss our Resurrection sale! 30% off!

"Subtle," Clarence says with a nod, watching as it flaps in the wind.

According to the lawyers, there's not much we can do when it comes to the upcoming vote. It comes down to the people and what they want. We have three months before the vote takes place and we've been trying to brainstorm ideas to get the public on our side.

Apparently satisfied with their plan to get Scarlet Toys shut down, the protesters have not resumed their usual daily march. They must be optimistic about the outcome. I wish I could say the same for us.

The looming threat seems to have a positive effect on business. Even after the sale is over, we have a steady stream of customers. More people are willing to shop with us when they don't have to cross a picket line. Plus, the controversy has reached the local news station, who did a story about the upcoming vote. You couldn't ask for better advertising. We've had customers from a lot of the surrounding towns as well.

Vote Yes on Prop 4 and *Vote No on Prop 4* signs appear like magic around town, in yards and the windows of businesses and churches.

"There seem to be a lot more vote yes signs," I point out to Wyatt as we sit on my couch. I'm sewing eyes on a bright blue stuffed dog.

"It does appear that way." Wyatt watches me stitch with a small smile. "What do you do with the stuffed animals when you've finished them?"

"When I get a box full, like thirty or so, I send them to the local Department for Family and Children. They give them to kids who are removed from their homes and put into foster care."

Wyatt stares at me for a moment. "Did you know someone in foster care?"

"No, I just like making stuffed animals and I have to do something with them. It's not nearly as philanthropic as it seems."

"Sure it is. You could be selling them."

"They aren't that good," I snort, tucking my feet under the edge of his thigh.

"Are you kidding? People will pay good money for handmade stuff like that, and yours are really unique." He rubs my knee.

"Thanks, but it's just a hobby." I glance at his computer screen. "What is the Lawson House?"

Wyatt shrugs. "A charity I started about eight years ago. We build community centers in run down areas to give kids something to do after school. Once this situation with Scarlet Toys is resolved, I planned to scout out a new location. I heard back from the publicist today, though. She's been brainstorming ideas to get the public on our side when it comes to the vote. Since they're claiming this is all about the children, I asked what she thought of putting the next community center here."

"That's a great idea!"

Wyatt frowns. "She thought so too, but I'm not sure. I usually keep these things separate. Are parents really going to want to let their kids hang out at a place owned by the local smut peddler?"

"Are you kidding? If you give them a place to park their kids after school without having to pay for a babysitter, they'll start marching with *Vibrators for Everyone* signs."

Excitement shoots through me, and I sit up and pull his laptop half onto my lap. "Tell me about the Lawson House."

He rests his arm over my shoulders and clicks on the website showing pictures of his community center. Pride emanates in his voice when he starts giving me a virtual tour. "There's a gymnasium with a basketball court, an outdoor playground, a game room with a ping pong table, Nintendo Wii section, and a place to play board games. This section is set up for classrooms, where the kids can meet with tutors, get help with their homework and stuff. I've been considering putting a pool in at the next one." He turns to me. "Do you realize a lot of kids who grow up under or near the poverty line never learn to swim? It's dangerous."

"Our county doesn't have a pool. I imagine most of the kids here have never been swimming." I peek up at him. "Isn't all this really expensive, though?"

"It's well funded by donations. People in my father's social circles are eager to give and get on his good side. He has a lot of influence among the affluent. They all try to one up one another on who gives the most to charity the same way they compete to have the biggest house or most expensive car. I've invested some of it, plus the interest it earns is more than enough to keep three centers running."

"That's amazing." As someone who scrapes by, just trying to keep my car running and the lights on, it's hard to imagine so much money.

"Maybe this is the way to go. Show the town we can be good for the community." He rubs his chin.

"I'd make it clear that the store is funding it though. Make them understand the center is dependent on the funds from Scarlet Toys. Might sway the vote. Assuming we could get the center up and running before then."

Wyatt sets the laptop aside and pulls me into his lap. "We?" he says with a grin.

Damn. This really doesn't have anything to do with me. It's his money, his center, his idea. "I mean, if you want my help, I'd love to be a part of it."

"Of course I want you to be a part of it." His lips leave warm kisses on the nape of my neck. "We'll start looking for a suitable building tomorrow."

"Mmm...sounds good. You know the rule if you mess with my neck."

I grab onto him in a panic when he suddenly stands. "Grab the Scooby Doo soundtrack. I'm going to unmask the monster."

Gah, I'm never going to live that down. "The monster usually turns out to be a crooked old man," I laugh. "I guess your monster does lean a little to the left."

Wyatt's phone rings and he groans, grabbing it from the table. I excuse myself to grab a drink while he answers. When I return to the living room, he's pulling on his shoes.

"The police want to show us the video from the night of the arson."

Well, there's a surefire way to kill the mood.

Wyatt was informed that the fire was indeed arson a week or so after it happened, but it wasn't a surprise. We've been waiting to hear back from the police about the parking lot video, and they finally called today to have us come in and view it.

"You can't identify the suspects?" Wyatt asks, as we're led back to a small room with a television.

"Not yet, but I don't expect we'll have a problem once we get their pictures out to the public." The officer glances at his partner and they both grin.

"What's so funny?" I demand. Nothing about some assholes torching Scarlet Toys is amusing.

"You'll just have to see for yourself, ma'am."

The picture flips on to show the parking lot as a nondescript truck drives past and parks just out of range of the cameras. "No shot of the plate," Wyatt murmurs.

When the men walk up to the back door of the store, the rear camera picks them up as clear as glass. "What the hell? What's on their faces?" I exclaim.

"As far as we can tell, Ms. West, black marker."

Wyatt's chest rumbles with laughter. "They colored in their faces with black marker? That's their disguise?"

The officers laugh and lay out two photos they've taken from the videos. Both men would be instantly recognizable to anyone who knows them, despite the fact they've scribbled over their cheeks, foreheads, and noses with a black marker.

"We're obviously not dealing with criminal masterminds here. We wanted you to have a look first and see if you recognize the idiots before we release the picture to the public."

Wyatt shakes his head. "No, but I don't really know anyone here." He peeks up at me. "Cass?"

I give the two morons another look, but there's nothing familiar about them. "No, sorry, but they're older than I expected. I figured teenagers or maybe my age."

One of the officers nods. "We're estimating they're in their fifties."

"Is there anything else you need from me?" Wyatt asks.

"No sir. We'll let you know if we get any leads."

Wyatt thanks the officers and we head out the door.

"That should be an interesting news story," I laugh as we climb in the car.

He smiles at me. "More publicity."

We don't have to look far for a building for The Lawson House. The old elementary school building seems to be perfect when we do a walk through. It's small compared to most elementary schools now, but it's equipped with a gym and classrooms. Wyatt thinks the auditorium could probably be torn out and converted into a swimming pool.

"This is going to take a long time, isn't it?" I ask, after he speaks with the realtor.

"The pool will be a bit, but the rest is actually in really good shape. I think we could have that half open within a month or so. I'll get a crew in to clean and paint. The old art studio would be a great area for the game room since it's so large."

Wyatt grins down at me. "We're going to be busier than a dog with two dicks the next few months."

"You have such a classy way of putting things."

"Speaking of classy," Wyatt laughs, pointing at the pitiful laundry room located at the end of our street. It's provided for the tenants, but the machines don't work half the time, so most of us use the laundromat in town.

It's apparently in use today, though. One of the women who lives on the far end of the circle bursts through the door, completely naked, and proceeds to saunter across the street to her apartment like she doesn't have a care in the world.

Neal comes out the door a few seconds later and starts shaking his head the second he sees our expressions. "No, no. Wasn't nothing like that. Mary threw her clothes in the washer, sniffed the shirt she had on, then just stripped off everything she was wearing and added them to the load. Smiled at me on the way out. Bat shit crazy," he laughs.

"Are you sure you want to stay with me?" I ask Wyatt, as we head back to my apartment. "Violent Circle is insane."

"It's growing on me."

Wyatt wasn't exaggerating. The next few weeks we really only see each other at night and in the morning. He spends his days at the future community center while I run Scarlet Toys. Things have been going well. Business at Scarlet Toys is still great, and the community center is coming along quickly. Apparently, when you have enough money to throw at it, construction projects can be done quickly, because the pool has already been dug and installed.

We hear back from the police about a week after the photos are broadcasted on the local news that they have the men responsible. The grand jury indicts them and both accept a plea agreement instead of awaiting trial. Possibly because the pictures of them and their ridiculous scribbled faces have gone viral and they're the laughingstocks of half the country. It didn't exactly bring the honor and respect they hoped to the little extremist group they belonged to. Obviously, some people have a real problem with porn. They were both sentenced to ten years in prison, and Wyatt is satisfied with that.

Wyatt and I are getting along, and I know I'm falling more for him every day. It's unreal how much I enjoy the little things with him, like snuggling up every night to watch our favorite show before bed, or our routine, good-natured morning argument over who gets the first shower. Between Wyatt and work, I don't think I've ever been happier.

Still, the upcoming vote looms over our heads. I'm not oblivious to the fact that all my happiness can be undone by a group of puckered up assholes.

Jani bounces into Scarlet Toys on her night off with a big box in her arms. "Hey skank, you had any weirdos tonight?" she asks.

"Nope. It's been pretty quiet. What is all that?" I ask as she digs into the box.

Standing up, she smiles and throws me a white t-shirt with Save the Scarlet scrawled across the front in bright pink letters. "I had them made. I was thinking. Wyatt's planning a grand opening for the community center? Like a little carnival?"

"Yeah, we're hoping it'll draw in the kids, get some sign-ups for swimming lessons, tutoring, and stuff."

"We should have an adult festival at the same time. You know, with adult activities."

"Pretty sure that'd be illegal," I snort.

Jani looks at me like my cheese has slid off my cracker. "I wasn't going to set up a glory hole, for fuck's sake. I was thinking about a kissing booth, maybe a lingerie fashion show, that kind of stuff. We could have it the same night so parents can drop their kids off at the center and come here while they're waiting."

I've never seen Jani care about much of anything except her mother so I'm surprised she's putting so much thought and effort into this. "You really like this job, don't you?"

Jani smiles and holds a t-shirt up to her chest to judge the size. "It's a lot of fun. And I don't want those prudes to win."

"Wyatt's working late at the center. Why don't you stop by and ask him about your idea? And show him the shirts. These are great."

Jani's beam practically illuminates the room. "I will."

A man approaches the counter with one of our new items, a talking vibrator. "Hi, I was thinking about this for my wife as a gag gift. She'll be forty this week. Do you have any idea what it says?"

The only phrase listed on the package is *Not tonight. I have a headache.*

"No." I grab a pair of scissors and cut the top of the package. "But let's find out."

Jani hands me some batteries and I install them. As soon as I turn it on, along with the low buzzing, a voice groans, "Again? Don't you have a husband?"

All three of us crack up, but it keeps talking. Every thirty seconds or so, it spits out a new phrase. "Help, it's dark in here! I knew I should've gone to college."

Laughing, the man nods. "I'll take it."

While Jani runs back to get him an unopened package, the vibe keeps going. "Ugh, aren't you done yet? I'm bored." It then proceeds to sing Ninety-nine Bottles of Lube on the Wall.

We're all nearly in tears when I shut it off and bag up his purchase.

"Would you like a T-shirt for your wife?" Jani asks, holding one up. "They're free."

"Hell yeah. I heard they're trying to shut you down. I'll be there to vote no," he informs us. We thank him, and he heads out, still chuckling.

"See? What job could be more fun than this?"

Jani offers to help me close the store, but I tell her to go, and she calls me a few minutes later. "Wyatt said go for it! He put me in charge of the adult festival." She pauses for a moment as the responsibility sets in. "Shit. What have I gotten myself into?"

"Please, there is no one with a more creative dirty mind than you. You'll be fine. And you know I'll help you."

"Ooh, we could bob for something. Butt plugs? Nah, that's too gross. Don't worry. I'll think of something. I've got to go. Mom's not feeling well tonight. Talk to you later."

She talks a million miles an hour then hangs up on me.

Wyatt is standing right behind me when I turn around and I practically jump out of my skin. His chest rumbles with laughter, and I shove him. "You scared the shit out of me!"

"Sorry," he replies, sounding anything but. "Was that Jani?"

"Yeah, she's really excited."

He swipes a lock of hair off of his forehead. "Do you think I made a mistake putting her in charge?"

My fingers wander up to play with the lock of hair as it stubbornly falls back into place. "No, she'll be great. I'll let you know if she tries to do anything too dirty."

"Good. I need a haircut. Any idea where I should go?"

I throw my arms around his neck. "I like it long, but if you insist, I'd ask one of the guys you're working with. I go to the salon, but most guys around here go to a barber."

His hands travel down to cup my ass, like they usually do. "I'd hate to have my masculinity called into question because I went to a ladies' salon," he teases.

"You know a barber won't offer you a manicure, though, right?"

His lips twitch. "Very funny. Nail hygiene isn't just for women."

"Down here it is. You're lucky if the guys aren't digging the crud from under their nails with a pocketknife." I slide my hand over his and trace the lines in his palm with my finger. "Your hands are the best of both worlds. Rough from work, but clean, with nails that don't grate my insides."

His laughter fills the room and he leans down to give me a soft kiss. "I swear I never know what's going to come out of your mouth next." He plants another light kiss on the corner of my mouth. "I love you."

"Now you're thinking of what you want to go into my mouth," I accuse, moving my hand down to his crotch. "I love you."

"You'd better."

"What? Sorry, I was talking to your cock. Of course, I love you too."

The room tips as he throws me over his shoulder. "That does it. I'm taking you home. You have another date with the paddle."

"Only if you want to wake up with your balls glued to your leg."

His deep laughter follows us out to the car.

Everyone's relationships are like this, right?

Chapter Seven

I've spent the last two days alone since Wyatt had to travel back to Indianapolis for another board meeting. He's due back late, but I gave him my key, so I don't have to worry about hearing him knock. A small grin spreads across my face as I get ready for bed. Maybe I'll surprise him. I have a set of skimpy lingerie that Jani got me as a gag gift last year. She thought it was hilarious because crotchless panties isn't something I'd ever wear, and the bra is so sheer, there's really no point in wearing it.

I quickly dress in the tiny scraps and step in front of the mirror, fully prepared to laugh at myself, but I have to admit, it flatters my lean body more than I expected. Wyatt will waste no time tearing it off of me.

Tomorrow is going to be such a big day. The carnival has to be a success if we're going to show the town that Scarlet Toys can be a positive thing for the community. I'm sure the prudes will object to the kissing booth and the lingerie fashion show, but they aren't the people we're trying to convince. Shoving a lamp up their asses couldn't get those people to lighten up. It's the reasonable people we want to influence.

With all of these thoughts and concerns bubbling in my brain, I'm surprised I fell asleep so quickly.

A tapping sound pulls me from a dream a couple of hours later and I look up to see a shadow standing over me. I really should've left a light on if I wanted Wyatt to see what I'm wearing. My voice is clogged with sleep when I tell him, "Turn on the light. I have something for you."

The switch is flipped and the room floods with light that makes me wince. My eyes adjust after a second, and pure fear floods through me. I jump to my feet and grab the heavy lamp from my night stand.

A man grins down at my barely clad body, but it isn't Wyatt. He's young, younger than me from the looks of it, and the expression on his face says he's struck the lottery.

"What the fuck! Who are you? Get away from me!"

He steps back, his grin fading. "Is this part of the scenario, Jade?" He takes another step towards me, and I cock the lamp back, prepared to bust his head open with it.

It takes me a second to realize what he called me. Jade. This fucker climbed through my window just like the last two attempted to do. Jasper is still using the hook up app or running another ad, apparently.

"I'm not Jade. You have the wrong apartment and you have one second to get the fuck out of here before I call the cops!"

His face pales and he darts for the window, clambering through. I set the lamp down and grab for my phone. Fuck it. I'm calling the cops again. I'm sick of this shit. And I'm going to tell anyone who will listen what's going on next door.

Before I can dial, my bedroom door flies open and Wyatt is standing there, glaring at me. Without a word, he stalks over and drops my house key on the table.

"Wyatt—"

He raises his palm. "Don't fucking bother, Cassidy. I saw the dude jumping out of your window. If you wanted to see other people, all you had to do was tell me."

My adrenaline is pumping, and I can barely hear over my own heartbeat in my ears. "You don't understand."

His disdainful gaze travels down my body, taking in the skimpy panties and transparent bra. "No, you don't understand. I don't fuck with cheaters."

I'm stunned by his response, and that he won't even give

me a second to explain. Whipping around, he stalks out of the room, and I hear the front door slam.

What the fuck just happened? In the last five minutes, I went from being sound asleep, to being terrorized by a fucking moron, to losing my boyfriend. My phone is still in my hand, and I remember I'm supposed to be calling the police. I don't really see much point since the guy must be long gone. I'll contact them in the morning and see what can be done about the situation.

Flopping back on the bed, I watch the clock on my dresser flip from 3:59 to 4:00. Four in the morning, and I know there's no way I'm getting back to sleep.

After all that talk about being together and finding a way to make it work, Wyatt just stormed out without even giving me a second to defend myself. I mean, I understand how it must've looked, but the way he looked at me, like I was the dirtiest piece of trash he'd ever seen, tears me open.

Part of me wants to explain, to call or text him, but I just can't do it. Living on the circle, it's not the first time I've seen that look, and it said all I needed to hear. He'll never really see me as an equal. I'll always be one mistake or misunderstanding away from being a lying slut.

Fine. He'll be back in his town soon enough, and if he thinks for a moment that this means I'm giving up this job, he's crazy. He'll have to fire me, because I'm not quitting.

I do my best to behave so I don't get painted with the same brush that everyone does just because I live in a poor area. I've never been the one screaming in the yard, or acting crazy, but all bets are off when it comes to my next door neighbor now. I'm about to go white trash on his ass.

Since I have plenty of time before I need to be at Scarlet Toys, I dig through my closet for the poster board and paint I stashed there last summer after I helped Jani make signs for a yard sale. No one is going to get the wrong window again.

On each poster, I paint a large arrow pointing toward Jasper's side of the apartment. The messages vary.

Lying asshole here.

Jasper aka Jade two windows over.

Looking for your booty call? Next window.

I spend the next few minutes attaching the signs to my windows. Finally, I put one on Jasper's window that reads; *Not sure if you're into P or V? Enter here and win the mystery genitals.*

I'm going to contact the police and the rental office, but after what I've been told in the past, I doubt they'll do much. In the meantime, this should show him I'm serious and keep people away from my windows.

My attempt to wallpaper the exterior of the apartments has at least kept me from thinking about what just happened with Wyatt, but as the anger and adrenaline wear off, those thoughts seep in.

I shouldn't care. It started as just a fling and even though we both wanted more, we had no idea how we'd make that work. It's better to end it now. He'll be leaving to go run his father's company before long and I'll be left here drowning in crazy as usual.

I'm supposed to meet some of the other volunteers at eight, but pacing around my apartment gets old, so I go in early.

As I'm getting in the car, Neal calls out to me and jogs over. "What the hell, Cass?" he laughs, gesturing to the signs on my windows.

"He's still doing it. I had some idiot in my bedroom in the middle of the night last night."

"Are you shitting me?" All the humor is gone from his voice.

"Nope. I'm going to talk to the rental office on Monday. I won't have time today."

"You didn't call the cops?"

"I didn't see the point. They'll arrest the guys who get the wrong apartment, but that doesn't solve anything. As long as he keeps telling them to use the window, this shit isn't going to stop."

Neal shakes his head. "This is bullshit. I'll talk to the office today. My address is one number off from his, and I have a daughter at home."

I hadn't thought of that. "I'll file a police report too."

Neal nods and heads home as I pull out of the drive.

It's early, so I don't expect Wyatt to be at the community center yet, but I'm still relieved when he isn't. The entertainment company is setting up the rides and attractions for the kiddie carnival, so I head to the refreshment area and start setting up tables.

Wyatt shows up a couple of hours later and stops in his tracks when he sees me. Without a word, he walks past me and starts to direct some of the other workers. Okay, if that's how he wants to deal with this.

Ignoring him, I hop in my car and head to Scarlet Toys, where the large tent has already been set up.

Jani takes one look at my thunderous expression and exclaims, "Oh no. What happened?"

"Too much shit to explain right now. Let's just get this stuff done. What can I do?"

"I thought you were helping Wyatt at the center."

I silently shake my head, and she nods. "Okay, well, then you can set up the table for the vibrator races. Just use the colored tape to divide the surface into two lanes."

Despite the turmoil in my mind, a snort escapes. "Vibrator race? Where do you come up with this stuff?"

Jani shoves a hose into a large plastic tub and begins filling it with water. "Don't you remember that video that went viral? Three friends crashed a prissy bachelorette party? One of the things they did was hold a vibrator race. It was legendary."

"I must've missed that one."

"The winner gets their choice of a free vibe or cock ring, so I'm thinking this game will be popular."

By the time I have the table set up and taped off, Jani has the tub filled and proceeds to dump in a bunch of little plastic boobs and penises. I recognize them as party favors from our bachelor party section.

"Bobbing for dicks?" I ask.

"And titties. I don't discriminate." She gestures to a couple of boxes filled with prizes. Along with sex toys and porn DVDs, there are also some tamer options like gift certificates to local restaurants and the movie theater. "Each dick and boob are

126

marked with a number. They get to pick a prize from the corresponding box."

A truck pulls in, and Jani drops the hose. "Ooh, the baked goods are here!"

"Do I even want to know?" I giggle, following her to the truck.

It's pretty much what I expect. Trays of cupcakes and cookies in every x-rated shape you can imagine. "Vagina cupcakes," I remark, placing a tray of elaborately—and I have to admit—realistically portrayed vagina decorated cupcakes on the table.

"Cuntcakes," she replies, as if I should've known.

Two boxes of cookies shaped like balloons are mixed in with the other items. "I hope these are balloons because if they're meant to be testicles, they have a serious medical problem."

Jani glances over at the box I'm holding and shakes her head. "They're meant for the kiddie carnival. Would you mind running them over to Wyatt?"

Shit.

"Um, actually, I'd rather not. We aren't exactly...speaking to one another."

Jani whips around so fast she nearly loses her balance. "What? You're fighting? Today? Tell me you're kidding."

"We're not fighting."

Jani releases a breath. "Thank fuck."

"We broke up."

"What?" she screeches. "We've been preparing for this day for two months! What the hell happened since yesterday?"

I focus on putting the cupcakes into neat little rows. "I don't want to talk about it yet."

Before Jani can demand answers, Noble and the rest of the guys from Frat Hell arrive. "The entertainment has arrived," Noble announces. He flashes a devious grin at Jani. "I might need a little warm up before manning the kissing booth, though. Jani?"

Despite her near meltdown a second ago, Jani doesn't miss a beat. "Clarence brought his Dalmatian. If you sniff her ass first, I'm sure she'll let you kiss her."

SHADE

Noble's friends burst out laughing, and Jani shows them where to get the kissing booth set up.

I spend the next couple of hours jumping from one project to the next, making sure everything is ready. At one point, I realize Wyatt's car is parked behind Scarlet Toys, so I head down the street to the kiddie carnival to see how things are going.

Everything looks great. There are little rides for the kids, a petting zoo, a bounce house, an inflatable slide, and plenty of little games to win prizes. The kids are going to love it. Wyatt has recruited the new people he hired for the community center to chaperone the kids and help them with the games and refreshments. They mill around, waiting for the moment we open the carnival.

The sweet smell of fried dough and cotton candy fills the air, but my stomach clenches at the thought of food. I've managed to block out the thoughts of what happened last night so far by keeping myself busy, but the pain is there.

I love Wyatt. I believed in all the plans we made, believed we had a future, and now all that is gone. I don't know what tomorrow holds, whether I'll still be working for Scarlet Toys or what, but I do know I'll be alone, and the thought makes my eyes fill with tears.

I knew I shouldn't have let things get serious. I'm going to miss him so much. For now though, I have to swallow it down and get through the day. With or without Wyatt, this town is better off with the community center, and that will be supported at least in part, by Scarlet Toys.

We still need the vote to go our way.

We still need to Save the Scarlet.

I don't know how well attended the kiddie carnival is, but the Scarlet Toys festival is a raging success. It's amazing how even the most serious adults cave and end up giggling like children when presented with the dirty games.

I'm supervising the Dick and Boob Bob game while Jani runs the vibrator races right across from me. Noble and Denton are in the kissing booth along with two of their female friends I don't recognize. For a dollar, you can get a kiss, right there in public. For five dollars, you get to go into the little curtained area for three minutes. It reminds me of being twelve again and playing seven minutes in heaven in a friend's closet.

When the crowd thins a little, I let another of the Frat Hell guys take over watching people bob for titties so I can walk around and see how the rest of it is going.

Neal sits at a table at the entrance, making sure no one under eighteen gets in, and hands out Save the Scarlet shirts to everyone who enters. A group of protesters march near the road, but no one is paying them much attention. Security keeps them far away from the patrons.

"How is everything going?" I ask Neal, taking a seat beside him.

"So far so good," he says. "I talked to the rental office before I got here and let them know we'll be filing police reports on Jasper."

Shit. I still need to do that.

"What did they say?"

"Same old run around shit."

My phone vibrates in my pocket. "Speak of the devil," I mumble when I recognize the apartment manager's number. I step behind the tent to answer it. Instead of the apology and promise of action I expect, the manager starts bitching about the signs I put up.

It's the cherry on top of my shit sundae of a day and I've had it. My voice rises higher with every word until I'm yelling into the phone.

"Oh, you've got a complaint? Well, here's my complaint. I have guys climbing through my window to fuck me because Jasper is running ads claiming to be a woman named Jade and inviting them to climb through his window. I'm sick of you dodging the problem. I ended up with a stranger standing in my bedroom at four o'clock this morning! Since you aren't prepared to do anything, you can expect a call from the police as well as the local news station. I'm done dealing with this shit!"

I hang up the phone and turn to find myself face to face with Wyatt. "Get the fuck out of my way!" I snap, stepping around him.

His hand grips my arm. "You didn't know the guy? He broke in?"

"Now is not the time, Wyatt!"

"Yes, it is! Tell me what happened," he insists.

I jerk my arm from his grasp. "No, the time to ask me that was about twelve hours ago. That's when you should have given me two fucking seconds to explain instead of assuming I was cheating. Because that's what trashy people like me do, right? Just stay away from me."

Noble steps around the corner, drawn by the shouting, no doubt. "Cass, you all right?"

"Fine," I reply through gritted teeth. "Do you need something?"

"Just looking for a chick to fill in for a few minutes in the kissing booth. Dina needs a break."

"I'll do it." Okay, so it's an immature, impulsive decision made only to piss off Wyatt. But in my defense...it works.

"The fuck you will," he exclaims, glaring at me.

"What now, Wyatt? You want to fire me? Make my day from hell complete? Then do it. But until you do, I have a festival to run."

Without another word, I stalk off beside Noble and return to the kissing booth. It's not that I mind kissing a few guys, it's no big deal, but it's not something I normally would've volunteered for. I'm being petty, I know, but if he wants to act like I'm some kind of cheating slut, then I'll show him one.

I can feel Wyatt's eyes on me when I return to the booth where Noble, Denton, and a girl named Stacey are standing behind a table. There isn't anyone in line at the moment so we're just standing around and talking.

"So, he still isn't speaking to you?" Stacey asks Denton. I have no idea who they're talking about, but I'm listening anyway.

"No, he's so uptight."

Noble scoffs, "Dude, you drew a face on his dick."

"You mean he drew a dick on his face," I giggle.

"No...I don't."

"Hey, I didn't put the googly eyes on!" Denton defends.

"Only because the glue wouldn't stick," Noble laughs.

"Whatever." Denton crosses his arms. "It still doesn't excuse what he did to me."

"I'm afraid to ask," I remark, sitting down and propping my feet on the table.

When Denton doesn't reply, Noble speaks up. "He switched his mother's name in his phone with Kelly's, his usual late night booty call."

"It's not funny!" Denton insists when I crack up. "I texted my mom and asked for a blow job!"

"But she thought it was me, so she said yes," Noble quips, and Denton punches him in the shoulder.

"Fuck off!"

My chest hurts from laughing at these guys. It's just what I needed at that moment. A girl approaches with a cute, young guy. Freckles dot his cheeks, which are already filling in pink. "Come on, Ron, if I'm doing this, so are you," the girl laughs.

She grins at Noble. "We both want three minutes."

Noble leans across the table, smiling at her. "Pick your person."

The young man smiles shyly at me and nods. "Her."

"I'll meet you in the booth," I tell him, smiling and retreating behind the curtain while Noble collects the money. I hear the girl choose Noble, and Denton's grumbling just before a flash of light blinds me.

The booths are just made of blackout curtains, so I can't see the guy, but I know he must be nervous. It's cute and I want to set him at ease. "Am I the first girl you'll kiss?" I whisper.

"No, but you'll be the last," a familiar voice replies before his lips crash onto mine.

Lust wars with anger as Wyatt's tongue slides into my mouth like it belongs there. I want him. I hate him. I love him. I kinda want to bite his tongue off.

Finally, I pull away. "What the fuck, Wyatt?"

His hand runs through my hair, and I close my eyes, grateful he can't see my response to his touch. "I'm sorry, Cass. I saw that guy jumping out of your window and it ripped my heart out. I should've given you a chance to explain, but I was so angry and hurt." He pauses for a second before asking, "Did he hurt you?"

"No, as soon as he realized his mistake, he was terrified, as usual."

"As usual?"

"Time's up!" Denton calls out.

"Let's get out of here and talk about this in the light. We're hogging the make out booth."

As we exit, I see the freckle faced boy follow Dina into the second booth. I guess her break is over. "Thanks for all the help, Cass!" Noble calls sarcastically as we walk away.

I flip him my middle finger, and we head over to a picnic table.

"What did you mean, as usual? This has happened before?"

Wyatt listens as I describe the situation with the neighbor. "According to the office manager and the cops, it isn't illegal to run an ad and tell someone to climb in your window. It's just that his apartment is connected to mine, so they keep getting the wrong window."

"We're moving out of there," he states. "I'll rent a house."

It takes a second for me to comprehend his words. "We?" I repeat finally. It's time to get something straight. I stare him in the eye. "*We* don't live there, *I* do. And I'm not going anywhere else. It might not be the best neighborhood, but it's what I can afford for now and it's home to me."

Wyatt grabs my hand. "We've practically been living together, anyway. I can rent us a place. You don't need to pay for anything."

I hold up my hand, cutting him off. "I appreciate what you're trying to do, but no. I'm not moving in with you—or anyone—for financial reasons. If I live with someone it'll be because we both want it, not because I need it. This isn't a fairytale and I'm not the damsel in distress you need to rescue. I can take care of myself."

Wyatt sighs and runs his hand through his hair. "I just want you to be safe, Cass. At least let me try to do something about the guy next door."

"I'm handling it. Neal and I are both going to file a police report, and I'll be going to the local news station if I have to. In the meantime, I'll keep the windows locked."

Wyatt shakes his head. "You're stubborn as fuck, you know that?"

"So are you."

His eyebrows spring up. "How do you figure?"

Maybe it's none of my business, but I can't help but tell him something that has been on my mind. "You keep fighting to win and take over your father's company. But whenever you talk about him or your responsibilities there, your whole body tenses up and you get all broody. It just looks like you're trying really hard for something that only seems to make you miserable." His thoughtful gaze meets mine. "I hope you get everything you want, Wyatt. I just hope you enjoy it once it's yours."

"Are we okay now?" he asks.

He pales a bit when I pause, and I can see how much he wants the answer to be yes. "I need to know that you won't always jump to the worst conclusion about me when something goes wrong. I may be poor, but that doesn't make me a slut."

His jaw drops open. "Cassidy...your income or neighborhood never entered my mind. I would've thought the same thing if you were living in a mansion and some asshole was climbing out of your bedroom window. I don't care what you have or where you live. I care about who you are. I love you." He squeezes my hand. "So tell me I haven't lost you."

Maybe I have been seeing this whole situation through a veil of my own insecurities. Wyatt has never treated me as less than him for not having money. But some part of me believes it makes him better. That's my issue, not his.

"I'm not that easy to get rid of, Wyatt. I will expect a nice, long date with your tongue tonight, though."

He gets to his feet and pulls me into his arms.

"Until you beg me to stop, or Scooby starts playing again."

"If you don't stop with that, I'm going to start referring to it as a Scooby snack."

His laughter draws the attention of everyone around us. "Oh yeah, that's going to stick."

"No. No it isn't. Forget I said that!"

Jani approaches us with a grin. "All made up? Great. Good. Fantastic. Because the minister from Hillside Baptist just walked in and I doubt he's here to race vibrators or bob for dicks."

George Hyland walks through the displays and games, taking pictures with his phone, as if we won't recognize him. He doesn't speak to anyone, but I see a few guilty looks tossed between the guests playing games when they realize he has seen them here.

Jani elbows me. "I've got this. Have your camera ready."

Jani walks over to Noble and whispers something to him. Noble grins at her and nods, abandoning his post at the kissing booth. "Any idea what they're about to do?" Wyatt whispers.

"Nope, but I'll bet it'll be memorable."

Stepping aside, I train my phone on him and wait. The minister stands in front of the tub of plastic boobs and dicks, frowning, as Noble walks by behind him with a large glass of water. Pretending to trip, he dumps the whole thing right on his head.

"Sorry, dude, I'm a little drunk," he slurs.

Jani rushes over with a towel. "I'm so sorry about that! Let me help you."

George snatches the towel and dries his face as Jani grabs a vagina cupcake from a nearby tray. "Here, have a complimentary cupcake," she insists, shoving it into his hand before he can get the towel away from his eyes.

Jani nods at me, and I take a few pictures, trying to hold back my laughter. It takes him a second to realize he's standing in front of the Bob for Dicks and Boobs game with his wet hair plastered to his head and a vagina cupcake in his hand.

134

Snarling, he spikes the cupcake to the ground. "Have your fun now. This den of iniquity will be closed down soon enough. And no one will hire a bunch of harlots who sided with Satan."

"Hey!" Jani yells after him when he storms off. "I'm only half harlot! On my mom's side!"

She rushes over to me once he's gone. "Text me the picture."

"What are you going to do with it?" Wyatt asks.

"The reporter from our local paper was here earlier, taking pictures and interviewing people. She asked me to send her any interesting photos or stories that might pop up later. I'd say the minister bobbing for dicks and holding a coochie cake qualifies."

"I thought you called them cuntcakes," I laugh.

Shrugging, she downloads the picture I sent. "Got to clean it up for the general audience, you know." Jani looks from me to Wyatt and back again. "Now go get dressed for the lingerie show. It starts in ten minutes."

Wyatt glares at me, and I shake my head. "Don't even think about going all alpha hole on me. Nothing I'm wearing is transparent." I give him a quick kiss on the lips. "I'll catch up with you in a bit."

I see him and Jani chatting as I rush toward the tent. I can't believe I let Jani talk me into this. At least the lingerie I'm wearing isn't too skimpy. Some of the other girls are wearing thongs, and barely more than pasties covering their nipples. My black lace, baby doll nightie is almost prudish in comparison.

Jani pops around the curtain behind the makeshift runway that's been made out of fuzzy red carpeting. Yeah, classy all the way. "Dina, you're up first, then Cassidy, then..."

Jani drones on, listing off the order, but I've tuned out as my nerves have taken over. All I have to do is walk to the edge of the carpet and back, then stand over to the side while the other girls do the same. We aren't being judged. It's just to show off the assortment of lingerie Scarlet Toys offers. And to bring in the men, of course.

When it's my turn, I step through the curtain to a scattering of applause and whistles, just as Dina did, and I see Jani smiling up at me from the audience. Okay, I can do this. No big deal. So what if Dina's big boobs jiggled all the way and mine would need a six point earthquake to move at all. Totally irrelevant.

I can feel my cheeks heat while I walk to the edge and turn to walk back. The woman who is announcing talks about the clothing and the sizes available, but I barely hear her. I breathe a sigh of relief when I take my place beside Dina. Sure, they can still see me, but the focus isn't on me anymore. It's on…Wyatt?

Wyatt!

With a big, cheesy grin, Wyatt struts down the runway wearing a tiny blue thong that leaves very little to the imagination. My mouth falls open as I stare at his completely bared, tight ass as he walks away, but it's nothing compared to his walk back. I don't know how he packed himself into that thong, but his cock looks ready to spring free and attack at any moment.

I cover my mouth to try to hold in the laughter, but it's a lost cause.

"What? You don't like it?" he asks, flexing and making me and Dina laugh until our eyes water.

"Wyatt, what the hell?" This seems so out of character for him.

He shrugs. "Jani talked me into it. Wait until you see Noble."

The show goes on to hoots and cheers while Wyatt and I toss Save the Scarlet T-shirts into the crowd. The announcer calls Noble's name last and he comes out wearing leather chaps and a ball gag.

"For the more adventurous customers, we have an array of leather and latex wear, along with bondage gear," the announcer says.

Noble nods at the audience as he makes his way to the end of the carpet, his ass hanging out the back of his chaps. He catches the announcer off guard though, by taking the microphone and removing the ball gag from between his lips. His gaze locks on Jani as he speaks.

"Have a look, ladies and gentleman, at what I had to do to

get a beautiful girl to go out with me. January—the girl trying to hide—dared me and I won. So, where would you like to go on our date, babe?"

January laughs, shaking her head. "Get off the stage."

"Yes, dear." Noble jumps down and walks over to her and the crowd cracks up.

"He just had to top me," Wyatt murmurs in my ear.

"Don't worry, you have a much better ass."

"Aw, thanks." He glances around. "Let's make our exit."

We sneak back through the curtain and get dressed. "I have to get back to the center. We're cutting the ribbon in a few minutes and I have to give a little speech. Are you coming?" he asks.

"I'll meet you there."

Jani is directing a group of volunteers while they break down the impromptu stage. "Hey," I call, jogging over to her. "I'm going to head down to the kiddie carnival if you've got everything under control here."

"I'm good. Noble said the guys will stay until we close."

"You know you have that boy wrapped around your finger, right?" I tease.

"Yeah, but that's not what he wants me wrapped around."

I grab my jacket from one of the tables. "Are you really going on a date with him?"

"I made a deal." She shrugs, then smiles thinking about it. "I never thought he'd actually do it."

"He's as crazy as you. Thanks for everything you've done to make this work. I'll call you later."

It's clear why the crowd was thinning at the Scarlet Toys celebration. Almost everyone has made their way to the community center for the grand opening. Hope swells inside me when I see a sea of people in Save the Scarlet T-shirts. I know they've also been giving out stickers and signs as well. Maybe we do have a shot at this.

I've arrived just in time to see Wyatt walk into the roped off area just outside the front doors. He taps on a microphone and everyone recoils from the feedback, but it draws their attention.

"Hi, in case we haven't met, I'm Wyatt, owner of Scarlet Toys." He gives the crowd a dazzling grin that could charm the pants right off of the ladies...and some of the men. "I'm not good at speeches, so I'll keep this short. I've only been a part of this small town for a few months, but I've grown very fond of it. Growing up in a large city, I've never seen people pull together the way you do, and I'm so happy that some of you have come together to support our cause, to Save the Scarlet."

There's a smattering of applause, along with a few grumbles.

"I know not everyone agrees, and I also understand why some of you may be a bit apprehensive, so I want to clarify a few things and maybe put a few anxieties to rest. Scarlet Toys is an adult establishment and no one under eighteen is allowed inside. None of the merchandise we sell is illegal and all of it can easily be found in similar stores around the country.

"Certain...groups have built this agenda against Scarlet Toys on the premise that allowing us to do business here would be harmful to your children. I understand that you don't want your children exposed to adult items which may confuse or upset them. That's why the store doesn't have a display window or any way to view the merchandise without entering."

He grins down at the crowd. "Scarlet Toys has nothing to do with children, but that doesn't mean I don't care about the needs of the children in your community. And that's what the new community center is about, meeting those needs. Giving the kids a safe place to go after school, to get help with their homework, learn new skills such as swimming and archery, or just hang out and play a game of ping pong in the rec room. All of these services will be available to every child in the county completely free of charge."

That gets their attention, and applause lights up the night.

"So, you're using bribery," a voice calls out. Of course, it's Minister Hyland.

Not ruffled for a second, Wyatt chuckles. "I suppose it looks that way. However, this isn't the only community center I've built and sponsored. A simple internet search will show that this is the third center, and in case you're wondering, neither of the other two are in a town with a Scarlet Toys store.

"My father, Adam Cavenite, instilled a sense of charity and compassion in my brother and me from the beginning, and it's my pleasure and honor to give back to the people who have given so much to me."

A rumble of murmurs and exclamations send a tremor through the crowd at the mention of the name Cavenite. They're as stunned as I was to realize who is addressing them. "More than anything, I want to stay and do business in your lovely little town, but either way this turns out, I respect your right to choose what you'd like your town to be. We're fortunate enough to live in a free country where our voices can be heard, so please, make your voice heard Tuesday and cast your vote on Proposition Four."

The crowd applauds again, and Wyatt flashes another heart stopping smile. "Now that all that has been said, I believe it's time to reveal the name of the center and let everyone in for a look around." Wyatt nods to a man on a ladder, and he pulls the plastic tarp from the sign.

The West Center for Families is written across the concrete in black lettering, and before I can even realize he named it after me, I feel a soft hand on my arm.

"You'd better marry that man, honey," Martha says, shaking her head. She gestures to a balding man bearing a soft smile beside her. "This is my husband, Herb."

Herb shakes my hand. "It's nice to meet you, Cassidy."

"You too, Herb," I mumble, but my eyes are on Wyatt, who is gazing at me with a devious grin.

"Complimentary pizza and drinks are available in the game room," Wyatt announces, and props open the door. "Please, come in and look around."

The crowd filters inside while Wyatt finds me, still nailed in place.

"Well, how did I do?" he asks with a smirk.

"Why…you named it West."

He slides his arm around my shoulders. "Yeah, well, I thought another Lawson House would be a bit narcissistic. West has a much better ring to it." Leaning over, he kisses my ear and murmurs, "You've worked just as hard for this as I have. I couldn't have done it without you."

"I love it." I turn and wrap my arms around him. "And I love you."

"And all it took was seeing your last name in three feet high letters," he teases.

"You do know how to seduce a girl." We walk toward the door. "They know you're a Cavenite."

His smile is sheepish. "Yeah, total name drop, but for a good cause. Hopefully they'll realize having a benefactor would be good for the town."

"If Scarlet Toys is shut down—"

"The center will stay," he replies, anticipating my question. "It won't be the kids' fault if their parents vote against it."

"I guess we'll know in a few days."

By the time we close the center and everyone leaves, it's after eleven.

"The rental company will be here early in the morning to disassemble the rides and get everything. I've hired a local company to clean up after them."

I glance around the dark, deserted parking lot and an idea grabs me. "So, we're all alone?"

"Looks like it," he replies.

"So, Mr. Lawson, in your years and years of experience, have you ever had your cock sucked in a bounce house?"

His deep laughter fills the night, and it occurs to me I could listen to it for the rest of my life. Maybe I can make it my ring tone.

I grab his hand and lead him over to the bounce house.

It's dark, but a little moonlight bleeds through the mesh sides of the inflatable castle. Giggles fall from my lips when I step inside and promptly fall on my ass. It's been years since I stepped in one of these and I forgot how hard it is to stay on your feet.

Wyatt flops down beside me, sending me a foot or so off the floor. Laughing, he pulls me back over beside him. "Not as easy as I remember," he laughs.

There's no part of this that's going to be the slightest bit romantic, but really, who doesn't want to have some fun sex once in a while?

"I'm sure I can manage." He glances around again when I unfasten his pants and pull them down. Usually, by the time I get my hands on it, his cock is rock hard, but he hasn't gotten there yet this time. I want to feel him get hard in my mouth.

I wrap my lips around the head and take the opportunity to suck all of him in for the first time. Groaning, he threads his fingers into my hair as he thickens between my lips. It's a unique experience to say the least. Crickets sing around us and the smell of popcorn and fried dough still hang in the air while I make him squirm and pant. I love how he reacts and how fast I can make him come this way, but that isn't what he has in mind.

"Stop, Cass. I want to come inside of you."

"No condom," I mumble, rolling his balls between my fingers and making him curse.

"I have one."

The next thing I know, I'm on my back with my pants off and my panties around my ankles. Naked from the waist down, he crawls up over me. My eyes fall shut as he kisses and licks my neck, his hand traveling under my shirt and bra to rub and pinch my nipples. He knows my turn ons, that's for sure.

Something rattles outside, and I sit up a little, glancing around. "Oh, now that it's not just my ass on display, you're worried, huh?" he teases.

"Yeah, because getting caught with your dick in my mouth in an inflatable pink castle wouldn't have been humiliating at all."

His lips return to my neck. "We're alone. Don't worry."

The groan that escapes when he slides inside me could have been broadcast over the radio to the whole town and I wouldn't give two shits. He feels so good, the whole world around me fades.

Until the squeaking starts.

Yeah, a little bit of advice if you ever want to try fucking in an inflatable bounce house. Plastic squeaks. Loud. And it also rubs your ass raw.

His eyes meet mine and we both start laughing. "We're

squeaking, not fucking," I giggle.

"I'm going to squeak the hell out of you," he replies, and then slams into me.

The plastic burn on my ass really starts to overpower the pleasure I'm feeling, and I know he's getting close. "I want to ride you," I gasp.

The squeaking fades as he rolls off of me, and I struggle to straddle his hips. I rest my hand on one of the corner bars for a second to catch my balance as I take him inside of me. Apparently, there's some kind of button under my hand, because when I let go, music starts playing.

Loud.

As if the Scooby Doo theme song wasn't bad enough, now we're fucking with "It's a Small World" blaring.

Wyatt's body shakes with laughter beneath me, and I lie on him, pressing my face to his chest while I try to control my own. After about thirty seconds, the music stops and we get control of ourselves.

It's hard to get any traction and there's nothing to grab ahold of, so I hook my feet under his legs and lean forward on my hands, dragging his cock out of me and back in. The angle is perfect to hit my spot, and I realize I can come this way quickly.

There's no more laughter as I fuck him, slow and steady. My orgasm is right there, so close I can't stop when I feel him stiffen and find his own release. "Cass," he calls, but it barely registers.

I hear him call my name again, but I'm so lost in my own bliss, I can't respond. When I finally come down from the high and find my brain again, Wyatt is staring at me with a strange expression.

"Cass, um..."

It's then I notice the flashlight, and the face peering through the mesh screen. "You kids get out here," a voice says.

All I can see is a peek of the blue policeman's uniform.

Shit on toast.

I scramble around, trying to find my panties, but it's too dark. I settle for pulling my pants on. The urge to laugh almost overcomes the humiliation I'm facing when I realize every move we're making is causing the squeaking sound again.

Wyatt stands and tries to pull on his pants, but only gets one leg in before losing his balance and falling, bouncing me into the air.

I can't help it. I burst out laughing and the cop calls out. "Come on now, out!"

"Sorry! I'm working on it!" I reply.

Leaving Wyatt to finish dressing, I crawl out and come face to face with the same cop who helped me when the guy was at my window, and also stood guard for us at Scarlet Toys. Wyatt climbs out after me.

You wouldn't think a guy could sound so nonchalant talking to a cop while zipping his fly, but Wyatt manages. "My apologies, officer. We didn't realize anyone else was around."

The cop laughs and shakes his head. "I heard the music and assumed it was a couple of teenagers trespassing. I assume this is your property?"

"Yes, sir."

"Okay then, you all have a good night."

Wyatt chuckles when I cover my face and groan.

"Hey, this was your idea."

"How long was he there?"

Wyatt's grin is devious. "Before you came."

"Oh god, don't tell me that. And my panties are gone. Some poor kid is going to be jumping around at a birthday party or something and find my panties."

Throwing back his head, he laughs and pulls me over to kiss my lips. "You fucking kill me, Cass. I'll find them."

He crawls back into the castle and emerges a few minutes later, waving them like a trophy. When I reach to take them, he pulls his hand back and stuffs them in his pocket. "Finders Keepers."

"Pervert."

"Said the girl who wanted to blow me in a pink castle that plays It's a Small World." His grin widens. "And we would've gotten away with it too if it weren't for that meddling cop."

"I hate you."

By the time we head back to my apartment, we're both exhausted, but the night isn't over.

As soon as I'm parked, I notice the moving truck out front and see Jasper carrying out boxes. He glances in our direction, then pretends he didn't see us as he loads up his stuff. My signs have been torn down. Only the tape lines remain.

"Cass!" Samantha calls, waving from her step.

Unlocking the front door, I turn to Wyatt. "I'll be back in a sec."

"Does nobody over here sleep?" he mumbles.

"Life on the circle."

Samantha gestures for me to sit next to her. "Looks like your signs worked. The office manager tagged his door with an eviction notice this afternoon. Guess he thought he'd move out in the middle of the night to avoid everyone."

Maybe I should feel bad for getting someone evicted, but I don't.

"I talked to his mother. She's pretty out of it...dementia. She's going to stay with her sister in Marion."

"That's good. I couldn't care less where Jasper goes, but I'd hate for his mother to suffer because of his stupidity."

"Yeah."

"I saw Wyatt's speech at the center. I think this is going to go your way. The talk after was mostly positive. Even the people who wouldn't necessarily shop at Scarlet, don't really care whether it stays or goes. But they do care about having a place to take their kids swimming and stuff."

I get to my feet and stretch. "That's what we're hoping." The people don't realize the center will stay either way.

"Well, you'll find out Tuesday, I guess."

"Yeah, the mayor has promised to come and let us know the second the votes are counted Tuesday night, so we don't have to wait for the news in Wednesday's paper. We'll probably have some friends over to wait with us if you'd like to join us."

"Sounds good to me."

Wyatt peeks out the front door, and I nod to him. "I'd better go. It's been a long day."

I'm almost back to my door when I turn and add, "Oh, and if you know anyone who needs a ride to vote Tuesday, let us know. We have volunteers to take them."

"Will do," Samantha calls.

Chapter Eight

All the hard work and long hours catch up with Wyatt on Sunday, when he wakes with a fever and severe sore throat. "Ugh," he groans. "I haven't had strep since I was a kid, but I remember this too well." His cheeks are bright red and his eyes are glassy.

"You need some antibiotics, then."

He takes a sip of water and winces. "It's Sunday, and I'm not going to an emergency room for strep throat."

It's not like he couldn't afford it, but he's stubborn, so I know he won't change his mind. "Here," I hand him two Tylenol. "Take these and I'll see if I can find a doctor open."

He swallows the pills and goes back to bed while I dress.

Neal's sister is a physician assistant to one of the doctors in town, and I figure it can't hurt to ask if he could put me in touch with the doctor. Maybe the doctor will just call in an antibiotic script.

Neal's little girl, Bailey, opens the door when I knock. "Hi, is your dad home?"

"Yeah, come in." She walks to the kitchen and returns with Neal.

"Hey, Cass, everything okay?"

"Yeah, well…not exactly. It's not an emergency or anything, but Wyatt's sick. He thinks it's strep throat so I know it's only going to get worse without antibiotics."

Neal motions for me to take a seat and sits across from me. "Yeah, that's nothing to play with. I had rheumatic fever when I was a kid because of untreated strep."

"He doesn't want to go to the emergency room for something that's not technically an emergency, and all the doctor's offices are closed. I wondered if your sister might be able to ask her boss to do something for him?"

"Absolutely, Dr. Kelley has seen Bailey after hours before." Neal grins at me. "And once she hears he's a Cavenite…"

"It's a name that opens doors," I laugh.

"This might take a minute. My sister is kind of weird. She's one of those people who swears by homeopathic cures. She knows not to recommend that stuff to patients while she's at work, but I guarantee that'll be her first suggestion."

He grabs his phone, and I turn to talk to Bailey while he makes the call. "You're getting tall. What grade are you in now?"

Her face lights up with a beaming smile. "Fourth. I'm the tallest in my class. It makes the boys jealous."

"I'll bet it does."

"I'm going to take swimming lessons at the new pool and Dad says I can go there for an hour every day after school instead of staying with stinky old Ms. Lilith."

I love how kids seem to have no filter. They just spit their thoughts right out. Ms. Lilith is an older lady who lives next door to the school and runs an after-school daycare from her home. I've met her, and stinky is as good a description as any.

"That's great! You'll have a lot of fun."

I tune back into Neal's conversation with his sister. "Yes, the guy who just opened the community center. Yes, yes." He sighs. "I heard you. Marshmallow root tea for his throat. I'll pass it along. Now, will you please call and see what Dr. Kelley can do? Thank you."

Neal hangs up and shakes his head. "If you want to hang out for a few minutes, she's going to call back."

"Thanks, I appreciate you doing this."

"Anytime. I assume you don't want to try marshmallow

root tea?" he snorts.

"Pass."

Sitting back, he rests his foot on his knee. "It's crazy some of the stuff she comes up with. It started with a guy she used to date. Any problem you had, he had an answer. Usually something like 'Go out and find a mushroom that grows under a stone, rub it under your toenails, then twist your left nipple in a counterclockwise motion and that will make your hair grow faster.'"

Bailey giggles along with me.

Neal snatches up his phone when it rings. "An hour? I'll tell her. Thanks, sis. Yeah, I told her about the tea. Uh-huh, colloidal silver, got it. Yeah, Bailey says hi. Talk to you later."

"Dr. Kelley will meet him at her office in an hour," Neal tells me, after disconnecting the call.

"Thank you so much. I owe you one."

"Nah, that's what neighbors are for."

I give Bailey a hug and head back across the street to tell Wyatt he has a doctor's appointment.

"On a Sunday?" Wyatt croaks, incredulous.

"Small towns are good for some things. Everyone knows everyone. My neighbor, Neal, hooked us up."

An hour later we're sitting in the deserted doctor's office while Dr. Kelley examines Wyatt. "Yes, sir," she says. "Pretty good case of strep there, plus a sinus infection to boot." She strips off her gloves and writes a prescription. "Antibiotic plus a decongestant. Should have you feeling better in a few days."

"Good, we have the big vote coming up in two days."

She smiles at me. "I'm voting against the proposition. There's no reason to shut down that store." Pausing for a moment, she adds. "I can give you a shot of penicillin as well. Works faster."

The expression on Wyatt's face makes me burst out laughing. "Are you afraid of needles?" I ask.

"No...just not a big fan."

"Come on." I walk over and hop up on the table beside him. "I'll hold your hand."

Wyatt starts rolling up his sleeve, but Dr. Kelley shakes her head. "It has to go in a buttock."

"Of course it does," he grumbles, getting to his feet and turning around.

He glares at me while I try not to smile at him bent over, his ass in the air. "Payback for that paddle," I whisper, and his lip twitches.

The shot makes him flinch, but he doesn't freak out or anything. Before he can get his pants up, I grin at Dr. Kelley. "If you think he needs a prostate exam or anything while we're here..."

She cracks up when Wyatt jerks his pants up and spins around. "No worries, Mr. Cavenite. You're a bit young for that."

Wyatt thanks her and writes her a check for fifty dollars over the amount she charged, a bonus for coming in on her day off.

I drop him off at my place and run to get his prescriptions filled.

There's a bit of a wait at the pharmacy inside the supercenter so I shop around a bit, grabbing some ice cream and Gatorade, the two things I always want when I have a sore throat. Two things catch my attention. The first is that everyone, people I don't even know by name, take the time to say hello and wish me good luck on Tuesday. The second thing that stands out and makes me grin from ear to ear are the amount of Save the Scarlet shirts I see. By the time I get his prescription and a newspaper, and make my way to my car, I've lost count.

It's a good sign.

Wyatt takes the medicine and crawls back into bed.

"I grabbed the Sunday paper if you want to read it," I offer.

He takes it while I go to grab us both a drink.

A loud, gravelly laugh makes me hurry back to the bedroom. Wyatt smiles and holds up the newspaper. The headline reads *Naughty Festival Draws a Crowd*. Under it is the picture of the minister that I took and texted to Jani.

Under the picture, the caption reads *George Hyland joins in the fun to support Scarlet Toys*. There he is with a vagina cupcake in his hand, standing in front of the sign that says Bob for Boobs.

They've blurred out the Dicks part of the sign, but it doesn't matter. With his hair soaked, it looks like he's been playing the game before enjoying an x-rated cupcake.

"Jani is my hero," I crow.

"She's an evil genius," Wyatt says. "They also covered the opening of the community center. It's under the fold." Yawning, he lies back and closes his eyes.

"Get some rest. We'll read it later."

He sleeps most of the day, only waking to take a drink, use the bathroom and go back to bed. When he wakes the next morning, I'm getting ready for work.

"Shit. What time is it?" he croaks. His voice is even sexier when he's sick, raspy and low.

"Ten. I left you a glass of ice water and your morning pill on the nightstand. I'll bring you some soup at lunchtime." He sits up as I lean to kiss his forehead. He's still burning up.

"I need to go check on the center. I might need to sign—"

"Nope. You're sick. I'll stop in and make sure everything is running smoothly. I called Clarence in to work my shift at Scarlet, so I can hop between them and take care of you. You're going to stay right here and rest so you can be better tomorrow for the vote."

Flopping back in bed, he grins at me. "I kinda like it when you're all assertive and commanding."

The covers twitch, and I shake my head. "Are you seriously getting a hard-on because I told you what to do?"

"Who can know what he's thinking?" He peeks under the covers. "He is a bit perky, though."

"Well, tell him to calm down. You're sick. Is there anything I can bring you before I go?"

"No, get out of here. Don't overdo it trying to be everywhere today or you'll be joining me."

"Yes, sir," I tease, pulling on my jacket.

"Mmm, I like the sound of that even more."

The day isn't nearly as busy as I feared, though if the number of customers we have at Scarlet Toys is any indication, the vote is going to go well. There are a few protesters out front, but everyone just seems to be ignoring them.

The community center is running smoothly for its first official day of operation. The pool isn't ready to open yet, but the game room is full of kids as soon as school lets out, and quite a few show up for the homework helpers club as well.

I'm stopped by so many people, wishing us luck, and promising to vote no. I'm trying not to get my hopes up, because I learned during the last presidential election that anything can happen.

I stop by my apartment at noon with a container of stew from the local café, and find Wyatt looking up at me with a sheepish, guilty expression. Samantha sits across from him, and Mallory perches on the edge of the recliner. A bowl of tomato soup and another with chicken noodle sit on the coffee table.

"Great minds think alike," Mallory says with a smile. "Samantha and I both brought soup when we heard he was sick."

"Thanks for looking after him," I tell them, trying not to laugh.

Both of them say their goodbyes, and I turn to him as soon as they leave. "I swear, I can't leave you alone for a second. You attract bitches like an all girl's school."

He holds up his palms. "Hey, they showed up when I was vulnerable and helpless."

"Uh-huh." I sit next to him and touch his forehead. "You're cooler, and you look better."

"I feel better." He grabs the container of chicken stew I bought him and starts to eat. "How is everything going?"

I fill him in on my morning while I eat my sandwich, dipping it in the bowl of tomato soup. "If you feel up to it, Clarence, Martha, and Jani are going to come over after work tomorrow night to hear the results."

"I'll be fine."

He recovers quickly, probably accelerated by the penicillin shot, and by the next morning, he insists on going to the community center. "I need to be there, be seen, and remind people to vote." He drops a kiss on my head. "I'll meet you at the courthouse at noon, okay?"

"I'll be there."

He looks so sexy in his Save the Scarlet tee and a pair of jeans. It's hard to believe I thought he was some stuffed suit the day I met him. He's much more at home in casual clothes.

Cupping my face, he looks down at me, and I feel my muscles melt under his warm gaze. "No matter which way this goes, nothing changes between us. We're going to make this work."

"I know." He nods at my smile and heads off to the center.

Of course, I'm still concerned. Whether the vote passes or not, things are bound to change. We haven't discussed the future or what will happen when he takes over his father's business. Will he want me to move to Indianapolis? I can't imagine he'd want to live here, or that it would even be feasible to run a billion dollar company from this little town. I've just been trying not to think about it until we see how the vote goes.

It takes me ten minutes to find a parking spot down town. Every spot within two blocks of the courthouse is taken. I've never seen so many people down here at the same time. Wyatt waits for me on the courthouse steps, but I hang back a little when I see he's giving an interview to the local T.V. news reporter.

I don't want to be on camera. I just want to get this day over with and try to figure out where we go from here. She finishes and follows her cameraman back to the van, so I make a beeline for Wyatt.

"Wow, I've never seen such a turnout for a local vote," I exclaim.

"The line inside twists around the main floor up to the second floor where the polls are," he says.

Protestors march up and down the courthouse lawn carrying their signs and chanting, but no one, not even the reporter seems interested in them. Of the people milling around, there are quite a few wearing Save the Scarlet shirts, but there is no shortage of those wearing Children First tees as well.

"Ready?" he asks, and offers his hand.

We enter and take our place in line. One thing is for sure, no matter which side of the issue people fall on, they're passionate about it, because they're willing to spend nearly an hour in line.

"Most of these people are probably giving up their lunch break for this," I point out as we near the head of the line.

"I thought of that. I hired the hot dog vendor and sub sandwich truck to give away lunches to everyone as they leave," Wyatt replies, taking a paper ballot and handing me mine. We part ways to go to two separate booths and fill in our *NO* bubbles, before stuffing the papers into a box.

Wyatt stops to chat with the mayor and makes sure she has his phone number to call when the votes are counted. "Absolutely, Mr. Cavenite. As soon as I know, you'll know."

"Thank you, and it's Lawson. Cavenite is my father."

She smiles at him like she's thinking about how he might taste.

"You're lucky I'm not the jealous type," I tease, as we leave.

"Yeah, like I don't see all the guys leering at you." He stops at the bottom of the steps. "Who has the late shift at Scarlet?"

I face him and wrap my arms around his waist. "Jani and Clarence. They'll be coming over after we close. How are you feeling? I thought I'd have a little bonfire, let the neighbors come, unless you still aren't feeling well."

"I feel fine. Invite whoever you want. It'll be a big celebration."

"So optimistic." His hands wander to my ass, and I swat them away. "I'm already the smut peddling town heathen, isn't that enough?"

"But you're such a sexy heathen."

We part ways again, and I head back to Scarlet. We have customers popping in all day to let us know they voted in our favor. By the time I leave, I'm in pretty high spirits.

Wyatt isn't home yet when I get there, so I take a moment to drag out my portable fire pit and set up some chairs. I let Mallory know about tonight's little get together and she promises to spread the word.

Wyatt shows up with some takeout food. "I figured you wouldn't want to cook since people are coming."

"Damn, you're too good to be true," I mumble around a mouthful of noodles.

"So ladylike," he snorts, which earns him a quick view of my chewed up food.

We expect to hear from the mayor by eight or nine o'clock, so when ten starts nearing, everyone is on edge. And I mean everyone. We have a huge group milling around the yard, waiting to celebrate or bemoan our fate with us.

Clarence shows up with Jani right behind him, but I don't recognize the car that parks behind her. Whoever it is sure isn't hurting for money by the looks of his car. A man gets out and looks around, his face drawing up like he just smelled a pile of dog shit.

Recognition sets in at the same moment I hear Wyatt curse. "Fuck. What's my father doing here?"

"Planning to dip himself in sanitizer, by the looks of it," Jani says. "He stopped by the store and asked for you. Should I not have told him where you were?"

"No, it's fine."

"Well, you've drummed up quite a bit of excitement down here, haven't you?" Adam says, grinning at his son.

"We're waiting on the results of the vote. There was a proposition to—"

Adam waves his hand and chuckles. "I know all about it. Figured I'd come down here and see how it all works out."

His tone of voice pisses me off. Wyatt is his son. He should be rooting for him, not hoping he'll fail.

Wyatt's tight-lipped smile betrays his anger, but he hides it well. "Dad, you remember Cassidy."

"Of course, nice to see you again." He looks around, his gaze stopping for a second on one of the frat guys, Trey, who is attempting to ride a child's bike through the yard. Attempting, because Trey has to be two hundred fifty pounds easy, and the alcohol content of his breath could probably burn down the tree he just slammed into.

Adam's eyebrow heads north as he regards Wyatt. "Is this where you've been staying?"

Damn. Make it sound like he's living in a garbage dump, why don't you?

Unfazed, Wyatt nods and wraps an arm around my shoulder. "Yes, it's Cassidy's place. Everyone here is really nice, and you're welcome to join us at the bonfire."

Before his father can reply, Wyatt's phone rings, and I see the mayor's number pop up. "Hey, quiet!" I yell. "This might be the call."

The night goes from cacophony to silence in a split second, and everyone gathers around Wyatt.

He hits the button to put the phone on speaker, and grabs my hand. Holding the phone out where everyone can hear, he says, "Hello?"

"Hello Mr. Lawson, this is Jessica. The ballots have been counted."

She pauses, and I squeeze his hand. So much rests on this moment. It's not just my future job, but my friends' as well.

"I wanted to call and congratulate you. We hope you'll continue to do business in Morganville for years to come."

The words have barely been spoken when everyone cheers, filling the autumn air with hoots and applause that can probably be heard across town. The phone gets jostled from Wyatt's hand as I jump into his arms, and he hugs me so tight I can't breathe.

"We did it," he says in my ear, before kissing me senseless.

For the moment, I let all my worries over our future and how we'll manage a relationship go and just let myself wallow in the elation along with the rest of the neighborhood.

Wyatt sets me down and looks around him at the dancing, excited people. "I told you. The circle had your back. You're one of us now."

"And proud to be." He scoops up the phone and thanks the mayor before hanging up.

I'd forgotten Adam was there until he reaches his hand out to shake Wyatt's. "Well, son, I guess you'll be taking over Cavenite Entertainment after all."

Wyatt looks around and shakes his head. "No, Dad, I don't think I will."

Ice runs down my spine at his words. What is he doing?

Adam's head tilts to the side, reminding me of a puzzled dog. "I'm not sure I understand."

"I appreciate the offer, but I think we know it's not right for me. Vince should run the company when you're ready to retire. I've found the place I belong."

That "I smell dog shit" expression returns to Adam's face. "You can't mean to live here."

"Maybe not in these apartments, but I plan to stay in town. I like it here." He grins down at me. "The woman I love is here, and as you can see." He gestures around the yard to everyone. "We have a lot of friends here."

Adam scoffs and rolls his eyes. "Your decision making skills haven't improved one bit."

Wyatt shrugs. "But they are my decisions to make. You're welcome to stay and celebrate with us."

His father stalks off, and I grab Wyatt's arm and drag him inside my apartment. "Are you insane?" I hiss, trying not to be overheard from the yard. "You can't give up your fortune!"

Wyatt's smile is calm. In fact, he looks completely content. "Relax, Cass, I'm only giving up the opportunity to run my father's company. I've been groomed for it for so long I've never even considered whether it's what I want to do. To be honest, going back to Indy to sit in an office all day with the goal of adding more money to our billions sounds like a nightmare. I don't want to be like him."

"Wyatt—"

His fingers stroke lightly down my cheek. "You made me think about what I really want, Cassidy. It's not more money or success in business, or to walk in my father's footsteps. I want to be around people who care about me, where I can relax and be myself." He glances outside where loud laughter has broken out. "And watch the Outside Channel with you."

"But..it's so much money, Wyatt. I don't want you to struggle like I have."

Laughing, he pulls me into his arms. "My trust paid off when I was twenty-four, and my investments have tripled it. I'm not dependent on my father or his business, but I do still own a stake in it, enough to be a board member."

He grins down at me. "You don't have to worry about me. I'm not losing anything. I'm only gaining my freedom, and the life I want with you."

A lump forms in my throat, and he plants a soft kiss on my lips. "Don't cry. I hate it when women cry."

"Then don't say such sweet things," I choke, wiping my eyes. "I love the hell out of you, Wyatt Lawson."

"I love the hell of out of you, Cassidy West." He wipes a tear from my cheek.

Jani taps on the door, making us both jump, and she shouts, "Hey, save the slap and tickle for later! We want to cut the cake!"

After flipping her off, I look up into his smiling face. "Are you sure you're up for this? You've only had a taste of the insanity of Violent Circle."

"Your friends and neighbors are great. I love the way you take care of each other. I'm happy to be a part of it."

"Don't say I didn't warn you," I laugh. Wyatt grabs my hand, and we go back outside. Samantha and Noble walk over, holding each end of a giant cake shaped like a—

"Oh my god!" Mallory shrieks. "Is that a butt plug?"

Yep. My neighbors made a butt plug cake to celebrate. If tonight doesn't wrap up what my neighborhood is like in a neat little bow, nothing ever will.

My neighbors are poor, and none of us would be considered sophisticated by any stretch of the imagination. They do dumb shit, break the law on a regular basis, argue in public, and I've seen way too many of them naked, but look at them now.

They're thrilled for us when there's really no benefit to them.

They came together to help us save Scarlet Toys because we needed them, and that's all they needed to know.

Money, education, and high-class upbringing doesn't

instill the most important things a person needs in life; compassion, love, and a sense of community.

Violent Circle has no shortage of riches there.

Epilogue

One month later

"I'll be there in ten minutes," Wyatt tells me, before I disconnect his call.

I was just getting out of a nice, hot bath when he called, insisting I get dressed and go with him somewhere. All he would say is he wants to show me something.

With a sigh, I drag myself to my room and throw on some jeans and a sweatshirt. The last thing I want to do is go outside in the cold now that I'm warmed up, and with wet hair to boot. My hatred of the cold isn't the only reason I'm grouchy.

I'm anxious because I'm pretty sure what he wants to show me is a house. It's not that I have an aversion to living together, he's been staying with me for the last few months and we get along great, but the thought of moving terrifies me.

I've always had to depend on myself and plan ahead to be able to survive. I've always saved money when I could, and I chose these apartments to live in because the rent is cheap enough that I can afford it alone.

There's a waiting list for Violent Circle, because despite its reputation as the slums, it is affordable, especially for students, single parents, and the elderly. If I move out, I can't just move back in.

I know it's what Wyatt wants, and why shouldn't he? He's loaded and he shouldn't have to live like a pauper because of me, but I have to look out for my own future. Wyatt is my boss, my job is already dependent upon him. It's not that I think we're going to split up or anything, but shit happens. If he meets someone else he'd rather be with, I can't have my income and housing be controlled by him or I could be out of a job and homeless overnight.

I don't think he'd ever do something like that to me, but I can't risk it. I've been thinking about it, and I've decided I just need six months or so. Six months to pay off the new car I just bought, and put enough in savings where I'll feel safe leaving the circle.

I trust him, but relationships fall apart all the time. I just hope he understands.

I hear his horn honk and quickly throw my wet hair into a bun, shove a stocking hat over it, and throw on my winter coat. All the time I'm rehearsing in my head how to explain my worries to him without making him think I don't trust him.

He grins up at me when I open the passenger door, and I swear, no matter how long we're together, that little smile, the one that shows his slightly crooked tooth, never fails to send a mass of butterflies through my stomach. I look forward to seeing it every time we're apart.

"It's not that cold," he laughs as I settle into the seat and point the heating vents my direction.

"Are you kidding? I think I keyed your door with my nipples. Besides, my hair is wet."

"This won't take long. I promise."

We're just a few minutes outside of town when he turns into a long driveway. About halfway down it, a beautiful house comes into view. It's everything I dream of having someday, a simple farmhouse with a wraparound porch and plenty of land surrounding it. It's set back from the road, with plenty of privacy, but close enough to town not to feel isolated.

My stomach knots, not just because I'm going to have to turn down his offer to move here with him, but because I'll have to deprive myself of something I want so badly. The little devil and angel on my shoulder are screaming in my ears.

Screw safety and stability! Look at this place!

Don't do it! Your apartment is better than a cardboard box if this backfires!

Wyatt is buzzing with suppressed excitement as he parks and we get out. He grabs my hand and walks me around the side of the house. "Whose house is this?" I ask.

"Ours," he replies, smiling ear to ear.

"Wyatt, I know we haven't really talked about officially moving in together, but—"

He stops in place, just in front of the attached garage. Hmm. The garage door is open, showing the empty space inside.

"I'm not asking you to move in with me," he says.

What? He just said the house was ours.

The garage door slowly descends and it takes me a second to process what I'm seeing. It looks like he has raided the stock room at Scarlet Toys because I recognize all those sex toys.

The sex toys attached to the front of the garage door that spell out four words.

Dildos, anal beads, vibrating eggs, and every other toy you can imagine display the words *Will you marry me?* in three feet tall letters.

All the breath escapes my lungs and my head snaps around to look at him. "Wyatt," I whisper. It's all I can manage. There is not one tiny part of me that expected this.

He's down on one knee, a ring in his hand, gazing up at me with that little crooked smile I've never been able to resist.

"You opened my eyes to what was missing in my life and showed me how much more there is to living than being number one. I thought I was happy, but I didn't even understand what true happiness was until I found you. I love you, Cassidy. I want to spend the rest of my life with you. Will you be my wife?"

Tears fill my eyes and I choke out the word, "Yes." I don't even hesitate. All the time I was worrying about the future, he was planning one with me.

My mind races as he puts the ring on my finger, then lifts me up and kisses me senseless. It takes a second for the hoots and cheers to reach my ears through the chaos of joy and shock raiding my brain.

When I'm back on my feet, I look up to see Jani, Noble, Clarence, and Martha ducking out of the garage and coming toward us.

I'm swept up in hugs and congratulations from all of them.

"You hooker!" I exclaim, hugging Jani. "You knew about this, didn't you?"

"Of course! And I expect to be your maid of honor. I don't help glue vibrators to a door for just anyone, you know."

I study their artwork again. "Did you dot the I with a buttplug?"

"That was Wyatt. He really seems to be into the butt toys. You should probably get a strap on."

My grin is devious when I turn to Wyatt and he shakes his head as I announce, "Oh, we already have one."

"That she has never used!" he insists. "My ass is padlocked, remember?"

Wrapping my arms around his waist, I lay my cheek on his chest. "You have the key to my heart. I have the key to your ass. It's fate."

"Not exactly a Hallmark card poem," Martha quips.

"He proposed with sex toys. You're in the wrong place if you're looking for classy," Noble snorts.

Clarence shakes his head. "The wedding should be interesting."

Wyatt wraps his arm around my waist. "Come on, let me show you the house." When we get to the door, he adds, "The furniture was included, but we can sort through what we like and what we want to get rid of."

Warm air rushes over us as we walk into the foyer, the others right behind us. Wyatt shows me around, and the place is beautiful. I can't wait to decorate it more to our taste and fill it with comfortable furniture.

I'm surprised to find a fireplace in the master bedroom as well as the living room. "We can lie in bed by the fire," I remark.

Wyatt's gaze settles on mine. "Do you like it?"

Is he kidding? "I love it, every inch of it, but not nearly as much as I love you."

Jani's laughter filters through from the living room where they're gathered.

An evil idea forms in my brain as I realize the timing is perfect. Grinning at Wyatt, I reach over and swing the bedroom door shut. I turn the lock and face Wyatt.

"Before we leave, there's one thing I have to do."

"Cass." He chuckles when I unfasten his jeans, but he doesn't object when I shove them and his underwear to his feet. I mean, what guy ever objects to a blow job?

He throws his head back when I wrap my lips around him and the way he stiffens tells me this won't take long. I give him all I've got, right up until I know he's on the edge of losing it. "My kinky girl," he gasps. "I think you like the idea of being caught."

"Or maybe." I stand up and take a step back away from him. "Payback is a bitch."

His mouth drops open and he takes a step toward me. "What?"

"When you least expect it, remember?" I unlock the door and grin back at him. "It's voice activated. Just tell it to come." With a wink, I step out the door and close it behind me.

Jani and Noble are snooping around the kitchen when I enter. "Where's Wyatt?" Noble asks.

"Pulling himself together," I reply with a grin.

Jani looks at me and her lips tilt up. She knows me. "What did you do?"

"I told you about the time he made me think he drowned?"

"Uh-huh."

"And when he made me talk to his toaster?"

"Oh my god. You finally got him back? What did you do?"

Hopping up to sit on the counter, I shrug. "Nothing bad. I just gave him the penguin."

Jani bursts out laughing, especially when Noble asks, "What the hell is the penguin?"

"When you blow a guy, but stop before he comes. He'll try to chase you with his pants around his ankles." Jani wipes her eyes. "Looks like a penguin."

I look up just in time to realize Wyatt is standing in the doorway, his arms crossed, fighting back a smile.

"Truce?" I offer, sliding off the counter.

He stalks over, making me walk backwards until I'm against the wall. His hot breath is in my ear. "You don't want to tell them what else you were getting revenge for?" he murmurs, and my eyes nearly pop out of my head.

The paddle. He'd better never tell them. "Don't you dare."

Chuckling, he steps back. "You can get reacquainted when we get home."

I throw my arms around his neck. "You still love me?"

"Always, baby." His lips find mine in a long, intense kiss, eventually broken by Noble's voice.

"Why the hell were you talking to a toaster?"

Thanks for reading! If you'd like to check out more of my work, I have two books that are always free!

Everly, Book one of The Striking Back Series.
And
Landon, Book one of The In Safe Hands Series.

Acknowledgements

This is the first romantic comedy I've written without a co-author. After hearing stories about my crazy neighborhood, C.M. Owens talked me into it. So ultimately, this book is her fault. On the condition that it isn't universally despised, she has my heartfelt thanks and gratitude.

To my betas, Veronica Ashley, Amanda Munson, Theresa O'Reilly, Bridget McEvoy, Lissa Jay, Chantal Baxendale, and Melissa Teo. Thank you so much for pointing out the embarrassing plot holes, mistakes, and typos, and keeping me from getting too ridiculous. I realize it was a full-time job.

The cover was created by Ally Hastings, who never fails to deliver no matter how picky I get. Thanks again, Ally.

I need to address all the ladies in the S.M. Shade Book Group. Watching you argue over my characters and claim them as book boyfriends (I'm looking at you, Colette) never fails to make me laugh. Thanks for making the group such a fun, drama free place to hang out. I love you filthy minded bitches.

Last, but certainly not least, thanks to all the book bloggers, page owners, and group owners who work tirelessly to help me and so many other authors get their stories out there. We couldn't do any of this without you.

Stalking Links

I love to connect with readers! Please stalk me at the following links:
Friend me at:
https://facebook.com/authorsmshade

Like my page:
https://facebook.com/smshadebooks

Follow on Twitter:
https://twitter.com/authorSMShade

Visit my blog:
http://www.smshade.blogspot.com

Sign up for my monthly newsletter:
http://bit.ly/1zNe5zu

Would you like to be a part of the S.M. Shade Book Club? As a member, you'll be entered in giveaways for gift cards, e-books, and Advanced Read Copies. Be a part of the private Facebook group and privy to excerpts and cover art of upcoming books before the public. You can request to join at:
https://facebook.com/groups/694215440670693

More by S.M. Shade

The Striking Back Series

Book 1: Everly

The first time I met Mason Reed, we were standing naked in a bank, surrounded by guns.

That should have been a warning.

An MMA champion, trainer, and philanthropist, but not a man who gives up easily, Mason is trouble dipped in ink and covered in muscle.

Growing up in foster care, I'm well aware that relationships are temporary, and I do my best to avoid them. After a sheet clenching one night stand, I'm happy to move on, but Mason pursues me relentlessly. Sweet, caring, protective, and at times, a bossy control freak, this persistent man has climbed inside my heart, and I can't seem to shake him.

After saving me from a life threatening situation, he's also won something much harder to obtain. My trust. But does he deserve it? Is his true face the one he shows the world? Or is his charitable, loving manner only a thin veneer?

This book contains sexual situations and is intended for ages 18 and older.

Book 2: Mason

From the moment I saw her, I wanted her in my bed.

I should've stopped there.

Everly Hall burst into my complicated life and changed it forever. I'm a fighter, but I had no defense against this beautiful, stubborn woman.

Now, I stand to lose everything I have, everything I am. My secrets are dangerous, and put more lives at stake than my own. I intended to tell her in time, but my time is up.

Everything rests on Everly.

This is the conclusion of Mason and Everly's story.

Contains violence and sexual situations and is intended for adults 18 and older.

Book 3: Parker

Hit it and quit it.

One and done.

Hump and dump.

That has been my philosophy on relationships for the last seven years. Don't get me wrong, I'm not a bad guy. I'm always upfront and truthful with the women I date. I don't promise them anything but a good time.

I could've gone on happily sleeping my way through the major metropolitan area if it wasn't for her. The dark haired beauty who haunts my days and keeps me awake at night. Strong and sweet, she makes me reconsider everything I believe about love.

Too bad she's completely off limits.

I've never been good at following the rules.

Book 4: Alex – An M/M Romance

Ninety- two days. Thirteen weeks. That's how long it's been since I lost my love, my best friend. It's been everything I can do to drag myself out of bed and get back to work, but I know Cooper would want me to move on. I think he'd even be happy if he knew who I want to move on with. The target of my affection, though, may not be so thrilled about my choice.

He's straight. Or he thinks he is.

A womanizer of the worst kind with a face and body that keeps a steady stream of willing women at his door, he seems happy to work his way through the entire female population. But there's no mistaking the way he looks at me when he thinks I'm not paying attention.

One way or another, I'll show him what he really wants.

This is book four of The Striking Back Series, but can also be read as a standalone novel.

Intended for 18 years and older. Contains sexual content, including sex between two men.

The In Safe Hands Series

Landon, Book One

Zoe

I'm not interested. I'm not interested in his blue-green ocean colored eyes, his lean muscular body, or that crooked smile that can be so infuriating. I have more important things to worry about, like how to keep myself in college and my sixteen year old brother fed and sheltered. We all know life is hard, some of us just learn that lesson younger than others, but that doesn't mean I'll give up. I intend to succeed and make sure my brother has the opportunities he deserves, and no privileged jerk is going to distract me.

Landon

I don't date. Don't get me wrong, I'm far from celibate, but my condition makes carrying on any kind of normal relationship impossible. My life revolves around In Safe Hands or ISH, the underground hacker group I work with to track down and take care of predators and sex offenders who beat the system. I'm satisfied with my life until the day I meet the smart mouthed, compassionate, determined woman who opens my eyes to possibilities I never thought existed.

Dare, Book Two

Ayda

I hear him.

His deep voice and rumbling laugh. The bang of the headboard slamming the wall and fake screams from yet another woman. Derek is a pile of muscle and ink, a bad boy fantasy only a few layers of wood and plaster away. It's all I expect or want him to be.

Until that irresistible voice begins talking to me.

Dare

I hear her.

The clicking of her fingers on a keyboard, her music or TV playing in the background. Her musical laugh and soft cries of pleasure, accompanied by a low, steady buzz. Ayda is a good girl who keeps to herself, and I have no business pursuing her, but I'm not a man known for doing the right thing.

I'm an ex-con. I'm a criminal.

And I want her.

Justus, Book Three

Justus

I'm not conceited.

Really, I'm not. It just so happens I have a body a Greek God would be jealous of, and a face that could make an angel weep. Other than that, I'm just your everyday normal guy who happens to take his clothes off for money. Sure, I've had to dispose of a few guys for In Safe Hands, the organization I work for that helps track predators and child molesters, but other than that, completely normal.

Women flock to me, screaming and paying for the right to touch me, so why is this woman so stubborn? Sadie Belmont's curvy body and sharp tongue have haunted me since I met her a year ago. There's something about her that gets stuck in my head like a bad song, and I'm determined to find out why I want her so badly, and why she can't stomach the thought.

Sadie

I can't believe I'm doing this. Of all the men in the world, I'm taking Justus Alexander to my childhood home in Oklahoma to meet my mother. A stripper who has a revolving door of women jumping in and out of his bed. Nine months ago when I lied to my mother and told her I had a steady boyfriend, I didn't expect it to come to this. She doesn't have long to live, and her only wish is to know I have a husband before she goes.

I can't disappoint her, and male escorts cost way more than I can afford, so when Justus volunteered, I took him up on his offer. I know what he wants. After annoying me with constant pick up lines for a year, he sees an opportunity to get me in bed. It's not going to happen. I just need to get through this week with my sanity intact.

Tucker, Book Four

Tucker

She's beautiful.

She's young.

She's driving me out of my mind.

I've always done my best to avoid Leah Bolt. I have enough problems without having to deal with a young woman with a crush. My life has been a disaster since I was court-martialed and dishonorably discharged from the military. After spending a year living on the streets, I'm finally starting to pull things together.

Now, I'm stuck with her, living side by side in my house with my complete opposite. If spending every day with this peppy, optimistic, energetic woman doesn't kill me, her brother

S . M . S H A D E

will. Dare is a friend and a member of In Safe Hands, a group that tracks down sexual predators and brings them to justice. He has also done time and is the size of a mountain.

I've survived combat, but I may be taken down by a perky blond.

He's gorgeous.

He's older.

He's a stubborn, broody jerk.

Tucker Long is every woman's dream...until you talk to him. He may be sexy when he's out sweating in the sun with sawdust clinging to him as he hammers and saws, but try to hold a conversation and all you get are grunts and nods.

He was the one who wanted a house sitter and just because his plans fell through doesn't mean I'm changing mine. My future is up in the air while I try to decide who I want to be, and Tucker's farm is the perfect place for me to do it. He calls me kid, but the way he looks at me doesn't lie.

I may be ten years younger, but I can still handle him.

All that Remains – An MMF Menage Trilogy

The Last Woman, All That Remains: Book One

When Abby Bailey meets former model and actor, Airen Holder, in a darkened department store, romance is the last thing on her mind. A plague has decimated the population, leaving Abby to raise her son alone in a world without electricity, clean water, or medical care. Her only priority is survival.

Traumatized by the horror of the past months, Abby and Airen become a source of comfort for one another. Damaged by her past and convinced Airen is out of her league, Abby is determined to keep their relationship platonic. However, Airen is a hard man to resist, especially after he risks his life to save hers.

When a man named Joseph falls unconscious in their yard, and Abby nurses him back to health, everything changes. How does love differ in this new post-apocalyptic world? Can three unlikely survivors live long enough to find their place in it?

This is the first of the All that Remains series and can also be read as a stand alone novel. It contains violence and sexual situations and is recommended for ages 18 and older.

Falling Together, All That Remains: Book Two

In the aftermath of a global nightmare, Abby Holder is living her dream. Married to the love of her life, Airen, and surrounded by friends and family, it seems she's found her happily ever after.

But the struggle of living in a post-plague world is never ending. When circumstances take Airen far away, she's faced with the devastating realization he may be lost to her forever. Broken-hearted, she turns to Joseph, her best friend and the only one who understands her pain. After all, he loves Airen too.

The sound of a car horn in the middle of the night changes everything, leaving Abby caught between the two most important men in her life. After surviving the worst the world could throw at them, Airen, Abby, and Joseph must face the most brutal human experience...true love. Can they overcome the betrayal, the hurt feelings, and jealousy to do what's right for the ones they love?

Their circumstances are far from ordinary. Perhaps the answer is extraordinary as well.

This book includes sexual scenes between two men and is intended for ages 18 and older

Infinite Ties, All That Remains: Book Three

The more you look to the future, the more the past pursues you.

Abby, Airen, and Joseph have fought and suffered to come together. All they want is to move forward and raise their family with the love they never had.

Unfortunately, the re-appearance of former friends and enemies complicates their lives, threatening to expose closely guarded secrets. With a vital rescue looming, their relationship isn't the only thing at risk. Can they let go of the past in order to hang on to a future with each other?

Made in the USA
Columbia, SC
16 December 2017